The Williams Sisters

The Williams Sisters

Connie Sieman

ReadersMagnet, LLC

The Williams Sisters
Copyright © 2019 by Connie Sieman

Published in the United States of America
ISBN Paperback: 978-1-949981-47-6
ISBN eBook: 978-1-949981-46-9

All rights reserved. No part of this publication may be reproduced, stored in a retrieval system or transmitted in any way by any means, electronic, mechanical, photocopy, recording or otherwise without the prior permission of the author except as provided by USA copyright law.

This is a work of fiction. Names, characters, places and incidents either are the product of the author's imagination or are used fictitiously, and any resemblance to any actual persons, living or dead, events, or locales is entirely coincidental.

Any people depicted in stock imagery provided by Getty Images are models, and such images are being used for illustrative purposes only.

Certain stock imagery © Getty Images.

The opinions expressed by the author are not necessarily those of ReadersMagnet, LLC.

ReadersMagnet, LLC
10620 Treena Street, Suite 230 | San Diego, California, 92131 USA
1.619.354.2643 | www.readersmagnet.com

Book design copyright © 2019 by ReadersMagnet, LLC. All rights reserved.
Cover design by Ericka Walker
Interior design by Shemaryl Evans

Chapter 1

Pasty and Mike Are Back

THIS STORY STARTS OUT IN THE ATTIC FACING the big window. The rain is pouring as the lightning flashed and it thundered. And all you hear in the background is the crying Peggy Williams. Peggy is having memories of her elder sister who just passed away that day. Peggy is in a full-fledged crying mode, and the front of her cheeks is so soaked in tears.

Standing in the doorway of the attic is her sister Pauline, who is also in tears. Pauline knows that she had just lost her elder sister Pasty. Pasty William, like Grand before her, is one of the best and most powerful among the good witches on this planet.

Pauline walks into the attic and sits in the chair next to her sister Peggy. The book of shadows is sitting on a podium in the attic. The thunder the lightning. Lighting up the sky different design like but it would light up the sky.

Peggy looks at Pauline and says, "We need to bring our sister back."

Pauline says, "How can we bring our sister back?"

Peggy says, "There must be a way to bring her back."

Pauline says, "There must be something in the book of shadows to bring Pasty back."

Peggy says, "Maybe we should have Grand help."

Pauline says, "We need to call Paul and have him come help us."

Pauline gets up out of her chair, and so does Peggy. Pauline opens her arms and says to Peggy, "Give me a hug. We both could use one."

Peggy says, "After the day that we had, yes, we could use a hug."

So, Peggy and Pauline hug.

Pauline turns around and walks toward the podium where the book of shadows is sitting.

Peggy says, "Wait! We need to light two white candles so that we can call Grand."

Pauline says, "Make that three candles."

Peggy says, "Three candles! Why three candles?"

Pauline says, "One for Grand, one for Mom, and one for Pasty. That's why."

Peggy says, "That is a very good idea. I knew you were smarter than you acted, Pauline."

Pauline turns and looks at Peggy and says, "Thank you. I appreciate that."

Pauline says, "I am so thankful, Peggy, that you don't treat me like a child. Pasty always treated me like she was our mother."

Peggy says, "You know, after Mom died, Pasty took the place of our mother."

Pauline said, "Yes, I know, I lived it. I don't need a history lesson."

Peggy says, "I did not want to give you one anyway."

Paul orbs himself to the attic where he finds Peggy and Pauline together. They were talking about bringing their sister Pasty back from the dead with good magic.

Paul says, "You must call the angel of destiny. His name is John Paul. You must call his name three times. He will appear after the third time you call his name."

Pauline says, "Okay."

Peggy then walks over to the podium where Pauline is. Peggy says, "John Paul, John Paul, John Paul." Then the angel of destiny appears. Peggy says, "Let's do a séance first and call Grand, Mom, and Pasty."

Paul says, "Good idea."

Peggy says, "Let me light the candles first."

While Peggy is lighting the candles, Pauline walks over to the book of shadows and starts to open it. Pauline finds the spell they are looking for.

Pauline says, "This is how you perform a séance, a ceremony to contact the dead. To perform this ritual, you will need six candles, white and purple in color, and a white cloth. In addition, you will need to sweeten the air by burning cinnamon, frankincense, and sandalwood. As the fires burn, concentrate on contacting the spirit and cast the spell that follows: If you are the name of this séances adjust the change accordingly. Beloved on known spirit, we seek your guidance. We ask you to commune with us and move among us."

Grand appears. Grand says, "My precious, precious granddaughters, I know what you need."

Peggy and Pauline say, "Grand, good to see you. We love you. We need your help."

Peggy says, "Grand, we must bring Pasty back! And we need your help."

Grand says, "Have you asked me to come in?"

Peggy says, "Come in, Grand. After all, this house was yours first, so of course, you're welcome to come in."

Pauline says, "Grand, I'm so happy to see you. Come and give me a hug."

Grand says, "You are my precious granddaughters whom I love very much. Tell me, how I can help?"

Paul says, "Hello, Grand. How are you? I'm glad to see you again."

Grand says, "Why, hello, Paul. How are you doing? I'm glad I got to see you again too. I see you taking very good care of my granddaughters."

Paul says, "Why, yes, ma'am, I am."

Grand says, "That's a good thing—my granddaughters before anything else."

Paul says, "You are correct, Grand."

Grand looks at Paul, Paul looks at Grand, and they hug each other.

Peggy says, "Where is Mom? We need Mom's help too."

Nancy appeared and says, "Good morning, my children."

Peggy, Pauline, and Paul all say, "Good morning, Mother."

Peggy says, "We need Pasty back. How can we do that?"

Paul says, "Peggy and Pauline, hold hands and call the angel of death. Remember, his name is John Paul."

Peggy and Pauline say, "John Paul, John Paul, John Paul."

Peggy says, "Hello, are you John Paul?"

Pauline says, "I'm glad you came to see us. We need your help.

Peggy says, "John Paul, we need to bring our sister Pasty back."

John Paul says, "You're talking about Pasty Williams, aren't you? We can bring her back, but we must bring Mike back too. Of course, it's up to Pasty and Mike if they want to come back."

Peggy says, "What do you mean Pasty and Mike want to come back?"

John Paul says, "We must ask Pasty and Mike if they want to come back."

Peggy says, "How long would it take for you to ask them if they want to come back?"

John Paul says, "Not very long at all."

Paul says, "Anything you can do to help, John Paul, we would appreciate it."

John Paul says, "Let me see what I can do, and I will be back to you."

Peggy, Pauline, and Paul all say, "Thank you very much, John Paul. We really appreciate all your help."

John Paul says, "Don't worry, I'll make sure that they want to come back. I'll make sure Pasty still has her power, so she can still help fight the good fight." John Paul then orbs back to the elders.

Soon after John Paul left, Paul is summoned by the elders. Paul says, "I must go and see what they want. I'll be back. I promise."

Peggy says, "I may be in bed by the time you get go to my room."

Paul says, "Hopefully, I will be gone that long."

Peggy says, "Well, it's almost midnight, so I may be in bed."

Paul says, "Okay, I'll see you in a bit."

Peggy leaves the attic and goes to the bathroom to get a wash rag and bring it to Peggy. Pauline turns around and walks down the stairs all the way to first floor and goes to the bathroom. Peggy then walks downstairs to the kitchen and opens the refrigerator and makes herself a ham sandwich. She makes another one for her sister Pauline too. Pauline walks into the kitchen, gets two glasses down at a walk to the refrigerator, opens the refrigerator, and takes out the pitcher with the tea in it. Pauline pours two glasses of iced tea and places a slice of lemon in each glass. Pauline picks up two glasses of iced tea, takes them to the kitchen table, and places them by the plates with the sandwiches. Peggy and Pauline both sit in the kitchen table, eating their sandwich and drinking their glass of iced tea while they wait for Paul to return.

THE ELDERS HAD ALREADY TALKED TO MIKE AND PASTY. THEY BOTH WANTED TO COME BACK so that the Williams sisters would be able to be the source of all evil. They could defeat the source of all evil if Pasty were brought back to life. The elders agree with Pasty and Mike. Pasty took John Paul aside and asked him to have a talk to Mike so that they could get married. Pasty asked John Paul to talk to Mike also about her being a good witch. She asked John Paul to explain to Mike why the Williams sisters had their powers and to make him understand.

John Paul said, "No problem. I can do that if you promise me something."

Pasty said, "What is that, John Paul?"

John Paul said, "You must promise me to always love and spend the rest of your natural life with Mike."

Pasty said, "I promise. I can pinky swear. You have my word." I will never forsake says: he will always love her.

Mike said he intends on making Pasty his wife. The elders said they can bring Pasty and Mike back, but they have another surprise for you and Pauline.

Holly said, "For heaven's sakes, what is the other surprise?"

The elders said, "You have another sister."

Peggy said, "Who is? What do you mean another sister?"

The elders said, "Grand will tell you."

Grand said, "Yes, my darlings, it's true. Your mother and two other men were dating at the same time, and you do have a stepsister. We don't know who the father of this stepsister is, but I can say it could be James and a man named Dave.".

Peggy said, "That is awesome! How do we bring these people back?"

The elders said, "Must turn back the hands of time. You will stay the same age you are now." Everything else will stay name the only thing it will be the timing you will work yourself back to where you are now soon.

Paul said, "Girls, get ready to do the spell to call a loss witch. You need to put the following ingredients in several mortars: a page of rosemary, a Sprague of Cyprus, and a yarrow root. Grind it with a pestle while chanting, 'Power of the witches rise, course and seeing across the sky. Come to us who called the near. Come to us and settle here.' Then spill the blood of the color into the mortar and continue chanting, 'Led to blind eye summons the blood to blood returned to me.'"

The moment those words were said by Peggy and Pauline, this glistening white light came over the whole attic. The light was so pure and so white and had sparkles in it. A soon as white light overcame the attic, Pasty, Mike, and Pamela appeared.

Now the angel of destiny said, "Peggy, Pauline, you have Pasty back. You three also have a new sister. Her name is Pamela Matthews."

Peggy said, "Thank you so very much."

As soon as Pasty, Mike, and Pamela Matthews appeared, the white light that engulfed the attic disappeared.

Pasty said, "Oh my god, Peggy!"

Pasty walked to Peggy and grabbed and hugged her. Then Pasty walked over to Pauline and said, "Come here and give me a hug."

Peggy then walked over to the angel of destiny and hugged his neck.

Pasty turned around and walked over to Pamela. Pasty stuck her hand out to shake Pamela's hand. Pasty said, "My name is Pasty! I am very pleased to meet you."

Pamela said, "I am very pleased to meet you."

Pasty said, "You are my baby sister, is that correct?"

Pamela said, "I don't know. I don't understand what is going on."

Grand said, "Nancy is your mother. Nancy is my daughter. Nancy and James are the parents of Pasty, Peggy, Pauline, and you, Pamela."

Pamela asked, "Is James my father?"

Grand answered, "We don't know who your father is. Your mother, Nancy, my daughter, was dating James and Dave. Dave is a white lighter."

Paul said, "A white lighter is someone who had passed away and was brought back to life to be a guardian new which is coming to powers. their magical powers. The elders gave you the white lighter power, Pamela, because they do not know who your real father is. Until we can do a DNA test on you, that will be the only way we can find out who your biological father is."

Pamela said, "So does that mean I'm a witch too?"

Pasty said, "Let's check and see."

Pauline said, "We will all have to say the invocation together. You are now in the wards of the witches and the secrets we hid in the night. The oldest of gods are involved here. The great works of magic is sought. In this life and in this hour, I call on the ancient powers. Bring your powers to be sister four. We want the power to give us the power."

Just like the first time when the girls the charm girls that will sisters received their powers the very first time the attic made up is pure bright light is absorbed the room, and it was so pure and so white. It was almost as if it was heaven sent. Just like before when they receive their powers the very first time, the house shook with all the force. But the manner with the shaking and trembling because of the powers that the girls the charm one will sisters was about to receive. These powers they were to receive were handed down from generation to generation of good and powerful witches who fought only for the good and looked out for the innocent.

As soon as the pure white light left the attic, Paul said, "Pasty, Peggy, and Pauline, please walk over toward me. Pamela, you come up here too."

Pamela walked over to Paul, where the other Williams sisters were standing.

Pasty said, "We need to redo the invocation."

Paul said, "I wrote one down for you, Pamela, so that you would have the spell and can read with the rest of your sisters."

Pamela said, "Thank you, Paul."

The Williams sisters said, "Here now the words of the witches. The secrets we hid in the night. The oldest of gods are invoked here. The great works of magic is sought. In this night and in this hour, I call upon the ancient powers. Bring your powers to us sisters or we want power, give us the power."

Just like before, when Pasty, Peggy, and Pauline received their power, the lights were twirling like a disco ball. The lights also flashed on and off multiple times.

Paul said, "Now you four witches have your powers."

Pasty said, "How do we know what Pamela's powers are?"

Paul said, "That's easy. Pamela, walk over here to me, please." Pamela walked over to Paul and stood in front of him. Paul instructed, "Pamela, hold your hand out in front of you. Call the candle on the table."

Pamela called, "Candle." The candle appeared in Pamela's hand.

Paul said, "Pamela's powers are of a white lighter. She can make things up here and her hand on my name."

Pamela said, "Paul, what do I do about the ringing in my ears?"

Paul said, "Hang on now. We'll get to that. The reason you have the ringing in your ears is you are a white lighter, and somebody is calling for help. That's what white lighters do. We help the innocent."

Pamela said, "So what do I need to do?"

Paul said, "You and I must orb up to the elders so that they can help you learn what you need to do."

Pamela said, "Okay, I'm ready when you are."

Peggy said, "I'm hungry. I need something, so I can feed my family."

Pasty said, "Yes, please, we are all very hungry. Please make some coffee to go with it."

Peggy said, "Not a problem, happy to do."

Pasty said, "I'm going up to the attic to look at the book of shadows."

Pauline said, "Peggy, can I help in the kitchen?" Peggy said, "Of course, you can."

Pasty walked over to Mike. Pasty said, "Mike, we must contact Darrell to let him know you're back."

Mike said, "You're right. You should call him right now. He is at home."

Pasty said, "I will call him right now and explain everything."

Mike asked, "Am I spending the night here? Where am I staying?"

Pasty said, "Of course, you are staying here with me. Mike, are you tired?"

Mike answered, "Yes, I am. I would love to go somewhere I can lie down."

Peggy said, "Mike, go upstairs to Pasty's room and lie down and go to sleep."

Mike said, "Thank you. I will do just that."

Meanwhile, Pasty, Peggy, Pauline, and Pamela ate their sandwich, and they decided they were going to bed. Rose went back to her apartment. Pasty, Peggy, and Pauline went upstairs to bed.

Paul went to bed with Peggy. Pasty went upstairs and slept in her room with Mike.

Before Paul went to bed, he went around and made sure all the doors and the windows were locked.

Next morning, Peggy was up by seven o'clock. She got out of bed and went into the bathroom, showered, dressed, and was downstairs making coffee when Paul woke up. Paul went to the bathroom, showered, dressed, and was on his way downstairs to have coffee and breakfast.

Shortly after Pasty and Mike were up dressed and went downstairs, there was a knock at the front door.

Peggy said, "Pasty probably Darrell you and Mike go hide in the laundry room, and please make sure that you shut the laundry room door."

Pasty said, "Aye, Peggy. Come on, Mike, ask of the laundry room."

Mike said, "Okay, let's go."

Paul said, "Peggy, you go answer the door. Take Darrell to the sunroom and then come get me after you tell Darrell that I have a very important thing to tell him."

Peggy went to the front door, and it was Darrell. Peggy said, "Darrell let's go to the sunroom. I have something I need to tell you, and Paul will help explain." So, Peggy and Darrell walked to the sunroom and sat down on the couch. Peggy said, "I have something very important that I need to tell and show you. Don't say nothing until Paul and I have explained everything."

Darrell asked, "Peggy, is everybody all right?"

Peggy answered, "Yes, as a matter of fact, let me go get Paul, and we can explain the whole thing. Just sit right here on the right, please."

Darrell said, "That's fine. I'll wait here."

Peggy got up and went from the sunroom to the kitchen, where she found Paul sitting at the table. Paul got up and knocked on the laundry room door. He opened the door, and he told them, "Come in the kitchen. I'm about to tell Darrell what's going on. I want you to be ready to show yourself to Darrell. I will let Peggy know when you guys can come in to the sunroom where Darrell and I will be."

Paul walked into the sunroom and sat down beside Darrell. Paul said, "Darrell, this is very hard for me to explain. You know that Pasty, Peggy, and Pauline are good witches. The angel of destiny allowed us the chance to bring Pasty back. We also brought Mike back."

Peggy got up with Pasty and Mike hand in hand. Darrell's jaw almost dropped to the floor in complete and utter shock, not believing what he was seeing and knowing that his partner and best friend who had died in line of duty was standing there before him alive and well and breathing.

Darrell said, "Oh my god, my prayers have been answered. Thank you, Lord. I'm so happy that you brought my best friend back, my partner in law enforcement. How are we going to explain this to our chief of police?"

Mike said, "I don't know how we are going to explain this to the chief of police, but I am ready to go back to work, so I would like it if you and I would go to the chief of police, so we can talk to him."

Darrell said, "Sure, I must go." Darrell stood up, walked over to Pasty, hugged her, and told her, "Thank God, you're back."

Peggy said, "I'm going in the kitchen and set the kitchen table for breakfast. I will let you know when it's ready."

Paul said, "Pamela, we are going to have to go to see the elders today. They have books for you to study your new power. The rest of the charm one I've had to learn on the job you will have the privilege Pamela of learning book learning also."

Peggy said, "You can do that right after breakfast, Paul." It did not take Peggy long to have breakfast served. Peggy said, "Okay, you all can come in here and have coffee and breakfast."

Paul said, "Good, I'm starved."

Peggy laughed out loud and said, "You're always hungry, but that's what you get for being a white lighter."

Paul said, "Peggy, trying to be funny this morning?"

Peggy said, "Of course, why not we don't have anything else, but he did it this morning right now that we?"

Paul said, "Now I guess not." Pasty said, "I need coffee badly!"

Pamela said, "You and me both, sister."

Mike said, "I will see you all later. I must go see my captain at the police department, let him know that I am alive and well. I don't know how I'm going explain this to him, but I will try my best."

Paul said, "Let me help you with that."

Mike said, "How are you going to do that, Paul? They have update had a policeman's funeral at the cemetery for me?"

Paul said, "Don't worry about it. The angel of destiny is going to turn back time. Just hang out here for a little while."

Pasty said, "Besides, you wanted to talk to Paul, you said."

Mike said, "Paul, can I talk you for a minute?"

Paul said, "Sure, I don't have nothing going on right now." So, Paul and Mike walked back to the sunroom where Mike told Paul that he wants to marry Pasty. Paul said, "Let's go together this afternoon. We will go to the jewelry store, and I will help you get an engagement ring for Pasty."

Mike said, "Thank you so much, Paul, for helping me."

Paul said, "No problem. You're practically family, and soon you will be."

Mike said, "I certainly hope so. I hope Pasty says yes."

Paul said, "Believe me, Pasty will not only say yes, but shall also be very happy and very excited. She will also want to set the date immediately."

Mike said, "Paul, you seem so sure of yourself."

Paul said, "Why, yes, I am. I already know what's going to happen. Remember, I'm a white lighter. Mike, I know who you are to Pasty. Pasty loves you the very same way. You may not be aware of this, but from each other almost my t devastated."

Mike said, "It almost killed me."

Paul said, "When you died, this whole family was very worried about Pasty. Pasty was very lost when you were killed. She killed the demon that killed you. When Pasty died, it made Peggy go crazy."

As Mike and Paul were talking in the sunroom, Peggy walked in. Peggy turned around and saw Pamela and told her, "Paul is waiting for you."

Pamela said, "Okay, I'm on my way."

Once Pamela walked into the sunroom, Paul said, "Okay, thank you, Peggy."

Peggy said, "No problem!"

Peggy walked over to Paul's hand, and they walked into the living room where Pamela is waiting for Paul. Pamela walked out of the room and because she thought that maybe Peggy want to give Paul a kiss, and she did not want to embarrass her.

Paul gave Peggy a kiss and a hug, and Peggy let go of Paul's hand. Paul said, "Take my hand, please."

Pamela turned and looked at Peggy.

Peggy said, "You'll be okay. You will be with Paul, remember?"

Pamela said, "You don't mind him holding my hand too, Peggy?"

Peggy said, "No, not at all. You must hold his hand."

So, Pamela took Paul's hand, and they orbed to the elders.

Pasty said, "Mike, you and Darrell and goes C / O with like, check and make sure you have not lost her job with the department."

Mike said, "Well, hopefully, nothing is wrong with my job."

Meanwhile, the angel of destiny changed turn back to when evil demon that had tried to kill Mike was back. But this time, Mike was there with Darrell Morris.

Pasty walked up to Peggy and said, "Peggy, you must, you must freeze him again. Pauline you wrote, so that we can read cast the spell."

Pauline said, "I still have that one from before."

Pasty said, "We're going to need it."

Pauline went to the book of shadows and looked up and found the wishing spell. Pauline wrote all three of them, so she can use them when it was time to cast the spell. Evil eye the, May the room extinguish be banned I will to the power of 4. I have earth, even and a cursed.

Pasty, Peggy, Pauline, and Pamela were required to say the spell three times.

Pasty said, "We need to say the same spell to get rid of the Tempest, and we will also need the spell that we used to get rid of shack, and it will take all four of us to say it four times to make the spell work."

Pauline said, "I have all the spells from last time. We had to do these spells before. Pasty, you remember that?"

Pasty said, "Yes, I do remember. I am so glad that we still have those spells, so we don't have to rewrite them. I'm getting hungry. Anybody else hungry?"

Peggy said, "Glad to hear that everybody makes my lunch for everyone."

Pasty said, "I hope were having leftovers, especially the leftovers from the whole week that we get them for lunch."

Peggy said, "Pasty, that's a very good idea. I think I shall go in the kitchen and start lunch."

Pasty said, "Walk with me to the kitchen, Peggy." Peggy said, "Sure, I would love to."

Pasty said, "I will go ahead and set the table. Should we use the dining room table or the kitchen table?" Pasty looked at Peggy.

Peggy said, "We might as well use the dining room table. Paul and Pamela will be back probably very soon. They will want to eat lunch also. Paul and Pamela will be very, very hungry."

Pasty turned to her right, opened the cabinet, and took out plates for lunch. She reached for the silverware drawer and got out silverware they will need. She took the glasses down for iced tea, and she walked over to the refrigerator. She got ice for all three glasses. She put the ice in the glasses and set them on the dining room table. Pasty then took the dishes and silverware and set them too.

Pauline walked into the kitchen and found her sisters smiling while they're working. Pauline said, "Glad to see you're all happy."

Peggy started warming the lunch. As each buffet dish was warmed, she placed it all on a counter next to the door that leads to the dining room from the foyer.

Once Pasty was done setting the table, Pauline walked into the dining room and poured the tea in the glasses that were half full of ice with a slice of lemon on the rim. Shortly after that, Pauline walked back into the kitchen and started putting the warm bowls of food that Peggy had warmed up from last night's dinner and last week.

Peggy said, "Come on, let's sit down and eat."

Pasty said, "Hold on a second. We should get two more plates and silverware and a glass half full of ice for Morris."

Pauline said, "Don't panic. Already done that. I'll set this up here so that when Paul and Pamela, over beside Peggy."

Peggy said, "Good idea. Glad to see you guys are on the ball."

Peggy said, "Sounds like Pasty and Pauline are looking out for Paul and Pamela. That's a good thing."

Shortly after the Williams sisters sat down at the dining room table, Paul and Pamela orbed into the dining room. Pamela said, "Wow, that was very cool."

Paul said, "I am starving. Please tell me there is food for Pamela and me."

Peggy said, "Of course, we're having leftovers. Please come sit and join us."

Paul said, "I want to wash my hands first."

Pasty said, "Paul, you know where the bathroom is. Help yourself."

Paul said, "Thank you, I appreciate that." Pasty said, "Anytime, brother-in-law."

Peggy smiled. Paul laughed, and then you smile. Paul walked upstairs to the bathroom so that he could wash his hands. As soon as Paul came out of the bathroom, Pauline walked in to the bathroom to wash her hands too. They both went downstairs into the dining room and sat down and had lunch with the rest of the family.

Pamela said, "I am so glad today is Saturday. I don't have the to work until Monday morning."

Pasty said, "Yes, thank goodness. Sometimes our magical situations can interfere with our jobs."

Peggy said, "Thank you, Pasty, for bringing that up. Later, Pamela I would love to talk to you about your work."

Pamela said, "All right."

Peggy said, "Pamela, if you want to stay with us, we have a spare bedroom for you."

Pamela said, "Really? Thank you! I appreciate that."

Peggy said, "Pasty can tell you that right now, we all live in the same room. It makes our powers stronger because we are family. We are sisters."

Pamela said, "I don't have a problem with that. I myself think it is very cool."

Pasty said, "I am so glad we don't have to add another room to the manor."

Peggy said, "That's for sure. We don't have to build another room and all."

Pasty looked at Peggy and started to laugh. Pasty then smiled a real big smile.

Pauline said, "Family is the most important thing we have in this life." Pauline walked over to Pamela and said, "We will help you move into the spare bedroom. All of us will help you with the spare bedroom, and you can park your car right here on the side of the road like we do our vehicles."

Pamela said, "Sounds like a good idea. Something for us to do today, on a Saturday."

Paul said, "I will help too."

After everyone was done eating, the kitchen and the dining room were cleaned. Everybody went to their bedrooms, got dressed for the day lighting up their vehicles and white Pamela's apartment. It took the Williams sisters all day to get Pamela into her room and empty out her apartment. After they were all done moving Pamela in her room, it was already nighttime. They were all very tired, and they were all sitting in the living room, resting and trying to relax.

Pasty got up and walked over to Pamela. She said, "I realize all this is probably very confusing to you, and for that, I am very sorry, but you are our sister witch, and yes, you do have powers. I realize that it's a lot for you to digest, but your powers are a gift, and your craft is something you will always be learning from books. and use of your powers. You must always practice your powers. You will do this by yourself and with your sisters."

Pamela said, "Good, I am very glad to have the help."

Paul said, "Pamela, you need to start reading all those books that the magic school let you borrow to learn your craft."

Pamela said, "Yes, I have a test in three days from Peggy. And three days after Peggy's test, I have another one from Pasty."

Peggy said, "We all should come to the dining room and have some dinner and go to bed early tonight. We need some good sleep."

Pasty said, "This will be the first time in a long time that we have all been in bed no later than ten o'clock, and it is Saturday night, no less.".

Mike said, "It will be good for us to get plenty of rest."

Pasty said, "Yes."

Peggy fixed dinner, and they all ate. Pasty, Pauline, and Pamela cleaned up the kitchen and dining room before everybody went to bed.

Paul said, "Peggy, I will be in bed soon. Make sure we are all safe from the demons and all criminals or, for that matter, all evil too."

Peggy said, "That is fine. I am going to get ready for bed and close for church tomorrow. I will also pick your out you."

Pasty said, "I'm going to do the same thing."

Mike said, "I will pick my out my suit her church."

Pauline said, "I am going to bed, and I am tired. Good night." Pauline then walked up the stairs to her bedroom and got ready for bed. Pauline picked up her dress, and then she took a shower. Just as Pauline started to get in bed, she had a premonition. Pauline went out of her room into the hallway. Pauline said, "Pasty, Peggy, page I just had a premonition." Pasty, Peggy, and Pamela walked out into the hallway.

Pasty said, "Can you tell us about it?"

Pauline said, "Yes, it involved Cole. He is back."

Pasty said, "Do we have a spell for him?"

Pauline said, "Yes, we do, but I don't know if it will work. I think we must have all four of us saying the spell together."

Pasty said, "I don't like George Mathis, and I do not trust George at all."

Pauline said, "I don't like him either, and I don't trust him too. If we can get rid of his evil powers, maybe we could save him."

Pasty said, "That is fine, but that will not stop him from trying to come after you use determine to have you."

Peggy asked, "What else did you see, Pauline?"

Pauline answered, "All I saw was called coming after you Peggy. He was throwing fireballs at you."

Peggy asked, "Why was he throwing fireballs at me? Why?"

Pauline answered, "I don't know, but I am going find out, and if Cole has intentions of hurting my sister, it's not going to happen. I will not let him hurt you, ever."

So, everyone went to bed. All the Williams sisters went to bed to get plenty of rest.

While everyone was in bed sleeping, Paul was making his rounds through the whole manor, making sure that all the doors and windows were locked. Paul made sure that all the floors, from the basement to the attic, were totally and completely secure. Paul went to all bedrooms invisible. That was one of the perks of being a white light. It was in the attic where he made himself visible again and set up crystals in every corner as a trap for any evil disturbing the manor. He raised his hand and said, "Activate."

When the crystal traps were activated, he made himself invisible again and went to his room. Once Paul made sure that the whole manor was safe, he decided it was time for him to go to bed too. Paul crawled into bed where his wife was sleeping knowing that the manor and the book of shadows were secure and safe. The whole family was sleeping peacefully and was quiet. It was a restful sleep that they all received. You have pleasant dreams and enjoyed every moment of their peacefulness.

Peggy set her alarm clock to go off at 7:00 am, Sunday. She got up out of bed, walked over to the end of her bed, picked up her house coat, proceeded to her bathroom to take a shower, put on her house coat again, and proceed downstairs. Once Peggy was downstairs, she proceeded to the kitchen, where she started a pot of coffee. She took the cereal bowls out and placed them on the counter. She took the silverware out so that she could put them along with the cereal bowls around the table so that she and her family would be able to have breakfast before going to church.

Then everyone was up and downstairs enjoying breakfast. Once breakfast was over, the Williams sisters headed back upstairs and got dressed for church. Paul and Mike went in their rooms also to get dressed. Peggy and Pasty had already picked out suits for Mike and Paul to wear. Once all the Williams sisters and Paul and Mike were fully ready, everyone went out to their cars and headed to church.

The Williams sisters and Paul, along with Mike, enjoyed being in church today. The sermon today was about loving thy neighbor. The sermon the Williams sisters hope and pray that their gifts would help the world. Once church was over, they all went back to the manor so that they could enjoy the Sabbath with their family.

As soon as Paul and Peggy arrived home, Paul had an uneasy feeling that came over him.

Peggy said, "What on earth is wrong with you?"

Paul said, "I just had a bad feeling. Come over here. I feel almost as if evil is near."

After Paul and Peggy arrived came Mike and Pasty. Paul and Peggy were standing on the sidewalk went through and Mike walked up.

Pasty looked at Paul and said, "What is wrong?"

Paul said, "Can't you feel it? Don't you feel evil in the air?"

Pasty stopped and was quiet. Suddenly, Pasty said, "I feel evil all around us as if they're out to get us, as if they want us gone."

Peggy said, "That is too bad. They cannot have us. We are not leaving. They will deal with this, and if they don't like it, that is just tuff."

Pamela had taken why out of the Jonathan and brought him to his mother. Pamela said, "Here, Peggy, take your son, Jonathan." Peggy took her son.

Paul looked at Mike and said, "Mike, come right here by me." Paul leaned close to Mike and said, "I want you to walk in the house with me. We need to check the manor."

Pasty said, "Yeah, that's fine, but what happens if the danger is out and you two are inside and we are outside?"

Mike said, "That is a very good point. I was just getting ready to say that."

Pasty said, "Sorry about that. I guess I just heard your thoughts, maybe."

Mike said, "I don't like the idea, Paul, of leading the girls, the sisters, out here in the open where harm can come to them. What happens if we were inside and the danger is outside, and we can't protect our family because of it?"

Paul asked, "What do you suggest?"

Mike answered, "I think it would be better if the girls are with us."

Peggy said, "I can have Jonathan to orb to his room and put his shield on him."

Mike said, "That's a good idea. Paul, our job as men is to protect our family.".

Paul said, "You are correct."

Chapter 2

Mike says: The first thing we should do is secure the outside. Once we have done that, then we are going read all of us go in to the house.

Paul says: That is a very good idea. I like the way you think of how to protect our family.

Mike says: It's my job. It's my family. I must look after them too. Can't just leave it up you.

Paul says: I'm glad to hear that. That will make my life easier.

Mike says: Paul, I would love to talk to you later in private.

Paul says: Okay.

After Mike had secured the outdoors now walked into the house, finding the foyer in the living room dining room and the kitchen fine. Paul says: I know it's safe downstairs. Let Mike and I make sure that the upstairs and the attic are secure.

Peggy says: That's fine with me. I would like to start dinner.

Paul says: What's holding up progress?

Pauline says: All the demons and ghosts busting we have had to do, and yet we continue to because the ghost the demons the evil beings will not get their heads to stop.

Peggy says: Pauline, it is okay. Paul and Mike, orb up to the second floor.

They proceed to check it out and make sure the second floor is secure and safe, and once they've done that, their next area will be the attic.

Paul says: Mike is going the attic and check it out.

Mike says: Open the door, and we will go in.

So, Paul opens the door to the attic, and what does Paul see? Paul sees the remnants of something in the attic. Question being what or who has been in the attic and why. The why was easy to answer. It had to be evil, whatever it was. The question is, what was it and what was a one and whom are the after? Paul says: Mike, remember where this was before?

Mike says: Yes, I do. I watched you when you put it on the table. Now how did he get on the chair?

Paul says: There is only one way that can happen.

Mike says: How?

Paul says: This is the remnant of a ghost or spirit. I don't know which one, but we're going to have to tell the Williams girls, and I will sister's things amiss in the attic.

Mike says: Our girls are not going to be happy over this. You do realize that, Paul.

Paul says: We still must tell them. It doesn't matter if they're happy over it.

Meanwhile, Peggy was downstairs with her sisters. She was fixing dinner. Pasty was setting the table and Pamela was putting it on the table in the dining room. Pauline was setting the glasses so that they would have iced tea when it was dinnertime. Peggy cooked a nice meatloaf with mashed potatoes, green beans, green salad rolls, and iced tea. For dessert, they would have leftover cake. Paul and Mike went back downstairs and walked in the kitchen and I walked in the dining room with a standing including Peggy Pasty looked at Mike and Paul and said: You act like you saw something bad upstairs.

Paul says: I did see the remnant of a ghost or a spirit.

Pasty says: Well, dinner is done, so we might as well go ahead eat dinner, and then we can go upstairs to the attic and check it out. How does that sound to you all?

Paul says: That works for me and Mike. Peggy says: Good.

Everybody sits down and gets ready to eat, and as they are sitting there eating, they are talking about the spirit that Paul and Mike saw in the attic. They decided that after dinner, when the dishes were all done, the girls would go to the attic and find the book of shadows to see if there was a spell to track spirits and ghost. About a half an hour later, dinner was done, the dishes were washed, and the kitchen was clean separate was put away everybody was ready to go to the attic when suddenly a spirit shows up in front of everybody. The spirit looks directly at Peggy and says: It is you I want and need. I cannot go on without you, I am in in the desperate need of your help.

Peggy says: Not on your best day, will you coming to my house that I come with you when I don't even know who you are nursing before my life.

The spirit said: You don't understand. I'm not asking you. I'm taking you, and there's nothing you can do about it.

Pasty steps up and says: Not on my life to come into our home and take one of us at you will or whim. Pasty says: she's looking directly at the spirit this is the Williams manor how do you walk float or whatever it is you did through our home without our consent or permission to do either are or.

The spirit looks at each one of them. She raises her right hand of your she has fire issues ready to shoot at them the only way that she will not shoot you come with him with her. Peggy looks are directly in the eye is do not shoot us we mean you no harm you trespassed in our home please leave our home without harming any of us. The spirit looks at Peggy and said: This I will do for you remember I will be back, and I will not take no, for a you have no choice. For now, you say your family.

Right after everybody was done speaking, the spirit that of course they don't know where the spirit went but if the spirit was not where they can see it. Pasty says: Come on, let's all go up to the attic. You would find out a little garlic the shadows you will find out there Pamela you can look in the shadows going into the attic please and if we find the spell to get rid of the spirit, write it down so we can all the all four of us together.

Pamela says: No problem. Happy to do it, anything to protect my family.

Mike walked over to where Paul was and says: Let's leave the girls to their job. I would like to talk to you in private.

Paul says: Okay, I will go downstairs.

Paul and Mike both walked downstairs and went into the living room, where Paul says: Is this private enough?

Mike says: Yes, this is perfect. Paul, I want you tomorrow after I get up or we must to go with me to the jewelry store so that I can get an engagement ring for Pasty.

Paul says: Sure, I'd be happy to help.

Mike says: Thank you, Paul. I appreciate that.

Paul says: Well, I am happy to have you as my future brother-in-law.

Mike says: Thanks, man, I appreciate that.

Everyone started heading to the dining room table when out of nowhere, they all heard a big thump that hit the floor in the attic. Pasty, Peggy, Pauline, Pamela, Paul, and Mike all jumped and looked straight up to the ceiling as if they were looking toward the attic. They all said: What the hell was that?

Paul says: Mike, come with me so we can find out exactly what's going on.

Mike says: Wait a minute, we can't leave the Williams sisters down here by themselves without any protection.

Pasty says, "Mike, sweetheart, love of my life, we are good witches. We are all able to protect ourselves. Please don't worry. Go with Paul and help him."

Mike says, "Oh yeah, that's right. You guys are witches, and you can handle things yourselves."

Pasty says, "That's right, we can handle things on our own down here, but Paul needs your help you to orb up there and see what's going on."

Mike went near Paul, Paul put his arm around Mike, and they orbed up to the attic.

Meanwhile, Pasty, Peggy, Pauline, and Pamela covered downstairs, checking it out to make sure it was safe and sound. Paul and Mike checked out that Paul discovered where the remnants of the spirit had been, he told Mike.

Mike says, "Don't you think we should go back to the sisters, no?"

Paul says, "Yes, I do. Let me go get the girls. You wait right here."

Mike says, "Good idea. I like the sound of that."

So, Paul orbs down to the dining room, where he saw all the sisters coming back from checking the whole house sure was a safe downstairs. Paul says: Everybody needs to hold hands, so we can orb back to the attic. We have something to show you.

All the sisters joined hands orbed up to the attic. Paul proceeded to show them working the remnants of a spirit in the attic. Pasty says: I found a spell in the book of shadows to get rid of the unwanted spirit.

Paul says: You might need that spell.

Once they were all done checking out the attic, they all held hands, and Paul orbs everyone back to the dining room to enjoy their dinner.

Everyone totally enjoyed their food that Peggy fix for dinner. Everyone told Peggy she was a great cook. Peggy says: Thank you, I am a chef. I went to school to become a chef.

Pasty says: Yes, you did, and now you're going to get ready to open your own restaurant.

Peggy smiled and said: Thank you.

Peggy says: I just paid off P3, the money I have made from P-3 I've also able to purchase, my new restaurant P-4. That is why I wanted to talk to you, Pamela. I wanted to ask you if you would mind running P3 for me?

Pamela says: Yes, I would. That would be so awesome. Thank you, Peggy.

Peggy says: I'm glad that you will help me, and I'm very glad that you will be a part of our family business. If the rest of the gang, we are good.

Pasty, Pauline, Pamela, Paul, and Mike were all in total agreement with Peggy.

Everyone was finally done eating. Peggy, Paul, Pasty, Mike, and Pauline got up from the table and walked back into the living room while Pamela cleaned up the kitchen and the dining room. Once Pamela was done with cleaning, Pauline and Pamela orbed back to the attic to see if anything else that happened. Pasty went upstairs to my room to finish her letter to her cousin. She had told her cousin Jack that she missed him dearly, and she wished that we would move back to San Francisco where he belong where the other two brothers were stay. Pasty also said: and her letter to her cousin Jack that they had powers magical powers, and she was wondering if Jack and his two brothers had that also. As soon as Pasty was done with her letter, she walked it out to the mailbox so that it would be picked up by the mailman that next morning.

While Pauline and Pamela were up in the attic, Pauline saw George Mathis up here. He was trying to talk to Pauline, but Pauline, refused to have a conversation with him. That is when Pauline and Pamela decided to go back downstairs. Pauline and Pamela knew that George Mathis would not have the courage to come downstairs to face Pasty. Pasty truly despise while the corruption of George Mathis her the evilness. Pasty always said: When you look, and Cole's eyes are you can see is pure evil. Once Pauline and Pamela were back downstairs, Pauline told Pasty what she saw. Pasty looked at Pauline. Pauline looked at Peggy. Peggy looked at Pamela, Pasty says: Pauline, why is George back?

Pauline says: I have no clue none whatsoever. I did not ask him to come back in my life. I would prefer that George Mathis would disappear forever, never to show his face again, but as you can see, that will not happen like that.

Pasty, Peggy, Pauline, Pamela, Paul, and Mike orbed back to the attic. Mike said: Pasty, back to work with you.

Pasty says: Of course.

She walks out of the attic in the hallway were Mike and walking with her toward her bedroom. Mike says: as Pasty and Mike walked into the bedroom please have a seat, I want to talk to you are you.

Pasty sat down on her bed, and Mike said, "I am so thankful that you and your sisters are back together again. I am pleased that you and I are back together also. I want you to know I love your family as I love you dearly, Pasty. You have been my first and only true love, Pasty. I understand that you have your magical gifts, and I do not have a problem with that. I am fine. You are a witch. I am proud of you, and I adore you. I love you, you must know that. We grew up together, Pasty, remember?"

Pasty says, "Well, of course, I remember. It's always been you and me in, I guess, everything. We've always been together. Apparently, you have some questions pertaining to that?"

Mike says, "You know me so well, Pasty. It's almost as if you know my thoughts."

Pasty says, "I feel the same way."

Mike says, "I just felt like I need to say that you fully understand what will happen later in the day tomorrow."

Pasty says, "That, like, it might be fun whatever it is?"

Mike smiles and says, "You're right. It is fun and can be very romantic. I hope you can handle that."

Pasty says, "Bring it on, big boy. Show me what you got."

Mike says, "Later, my sweet."

Mike turned around and took Pasty's hand, and they walked back to the attic.

Paul says, "Okay, Pasty and Mike are back. I wanted to let you guys know that I have found the remnants of two evil beings here in the attic while we were downstairs in the dining room eating dinner that was what the was the thump in the attic as we were getting ready to sit down and eat. The two apparitions that I have found the remnants of one is a spirit, the other is the evil demon name George Mathis who is the sources evil demon. Don't worry about that. We will catch them in our trap from the crystals that we have set in motion."

Peggy says, "We should all go back downstairs and have dessert. It's getting late, and we all need rest. We must work tomorrow."

S, Pasty, Mike, Peggy, Paul, and Pauline all walked downstairs to the dining room so that they can have cake for dessert and get ready for bed. Peggy started making decaf coffee and getting the saucers out and take you site everyone. Pasty took each individual saucer and set them on the dining room table with the cake arty slicing on the saucer Peggy put works on the sides of the saucers so that everyone will be able to enjoy their cake. Pamela sends out coffee cups around the table so that everyone would be able to enjoy the coffee and cake. Once it was all set and everybody was sitting at the table eating, they decided that they wouldn't discuss anymore the demon situation until tomorrow after work. Once Paul was done eating his cake and drinking his coffee, he orbs back up to the attic to check and to make sure everything was okay. While he was upstairs, he set the alarms and major the windows and everything was locked to the house would be safe.

Once the rest of the family was done eating cake and drinking coffee, they all brought the dishes in the kitchen and down the side the kitchen sink and they all went to their rooms to get ready for bed crawled in bed for what the night. Paul ordered downstairs to the kitchen cleaned up the kitchen white down the dining room table took the trash out, check the rest of the house downstairs nature all the windows and doors were locked turned out all lights went upstairs to his room and went to bed.

While everybody was in bed sleeping, the house was quiet. The only sound you heard from the house was the sound of deep, restful sleep. The dreams were sweet the rest with well wanted and needed the temperature was cool just cool enough where you want to have a blanket on your bed to keep you nice and cozy warm. Peggy had set her alarm to the for 7:30 a.m. She did not have to be at work until 9:30 a.m. Mike didn't have to be up until 5:00 a.m. because he had to be at work by seven to start the shift. Paul didn't have to be up until seven thirty or seven forty-five because he did not have a job as of late. Paul had heard that they were hiring at the magical school, and he was applying as a teacher. He didn't want to say anything to Peggy because he did not want to spoil it something did not work out. So, as they lie in bed, cozy, peaceful, and happy, resting in silence, evil was everywhere watching and talking about what their next plan is and how to get rid of the Williams sisters.

That was evil job evil was to get rid of all good witches. And all good which is new that was what enables job was to in all witches. The Williams sisters was learning their crafts, understanding magic, and accepting their gifts. As each day passes, they will learn understand and comprehend why they are going to be no as the Williams sisters what the name means. As the morning to break happens to break Peggy's alarm clock is all. It is seven thirty in the morning, a beautiful Monday morning. The sun is breaking, the birds are chirping, the squirrels are playing, and the bees are buzzing. Our girl's day is starting. Peggy is up and in the shower. Pasty is up and in the shower. She gets done with her shower for and they go on and get dressed because they know that they must go to work. Pauline and Pamela, you also they get their showers to start their day they get dress and that all congregates in the kitchen and while they are congregating kitchen, they smell copy and see bowls set out for cereal sitting on the counter waiting to go to the kitchen table. Soon everyone was at the dining table to have coffee and breakfast. This took about a half-hour. Once everybody was done eating, they left for work, and Paul cleaned up the kitchen. He took a shower and dressed for work. Paul had to report to the magic school as some magical children with their powers learning how to use their powers and understanding them.

The elders, I talked to a Cupid goal is known as Carl Manning, a bout Pauline. The elders wanted to fall in love with Pauline. They knew that Carl Manning would be perfect for her. The elders proclaimed it in the stars, that Pauline would fall in love head over heels with Carl Manning.

Carl Manning agrees with the elders to spend time and get to know Pauline. Pauline deserves to be loved to. Meanwhile, Pamela had met a young man who was a police officer who worked with probationary individuals. In other words, this young man Jack Marble was a probation officer who was a police officer also. Love was all around the Williams sisters. Finally, the Williams sisters would be able to find all of that you, if love was in the air.

While everyone was at work, the spirit that was looking for Peggy to be a companion with, was making her way through the Williams sisters' home. This spirit, the apparition, intended to make Peggy hers. This spirit was the pride of companionship this spirit was evil through and through and thought that if she could turn Peggy to evil that that would the Williams sisters. This spirit, of course, would be sadly mistaken. This spirit would have no chance of ever-changing Peggy from good to evil.

After Pasty went to lunch, she stopped by a wedding dress shop, looking for the perfect dress.

Chapter 3

THE PERFECT WEDDING DRESS FOR HER SPECIAL DAY. Pasty found two dresses that she really liked she decided that she would wait until this evening and call Peggy and have her meet her at the dress shop. While Peggy was on her way to the dress shop to be Pasty, Peggy called Pamela and reminded to not forget to turn in the notice can be working for me. Pamela said: Don't worry. I've arty done. I will meet you at home.

Peggy says: Pasty and I will see you there. Wait a minute, Pamela, are you off work already?

Pamela said: Yes, I'm just getting ready to leave work.

Peggy says: Me to meet Pasty and I at the wedding dress store in town you know the one only about my restaurant.

Pamela said: I am on my way to meet you there in fifteen minutes, if traffic is not a bear.

Peggy says: We will wait for you.

Pamela left work and headed to the wedding dress shop. She arrived, and they all looked around in the shop when Peggy says: Why don't you wear Mom's dress.

Pasty says: That is a good idea.

Once Pasty decided she would wear her mother's dress to her wedding, that is when Pasty, Peggy, and Pamela went home to the manor.

Pasty, Peggy, and Pamela arrived home. Peggy says: Oh, I must use the bathroom so bad.

Pasty says: Run, Peggy, run! Don't you have an accident.

Peggy says: I hope the house isn't locked.

Pamela orbed in to the house in front of the front door. She opened it for Peggy, and Peggy ran into the house and into the bathroom.

Once Peggy was done, she went upstairs to change her clothes, so she would be more comfortable.

Peggy headed to the kitchen to make sure the chicken was thawed out, so Paul and Mike could cook it on the grill.

It was about that time when Paul and Pauline came home from work. Pauline says: Peggy, what are we having for supper?

Peggy says: Barbecue chicken, baked potatoes, green salad, garlic toast, and tea to drink.

Pauline says: That sounds wonderful because I am starving.

It wasn't long after Paul for work at the magic school, when Paul orbed to his bedroom to get a shower and change his clothes. Paul cleaned up the bathroom after taking a shower and getting dressed for the evening. Once Paul was done with shower and cleaning up the bathroom, he then headed back downstairs so he can join his family to eat dinner.

Paul always tried his best to help with all the housework and keeping the house clean. He knew that would make the Williams sisters very happy. Paul always took pride in cleaning the house and the yard to help his wife and her family. Paul was a very honorable man. They all work outside of home, so they all had to work together to maintain the manor in which it was accustomed to. That was one of the things that Grand always wanted—her house cleaned, and her yard taken care of. Paul felt it was his duty as Peggy's husband to help in any way he could possibly help.

After everyone ate dinner, they all retired early because they were tired, and they worked very hard that day.

Peggy set her alarm to go off at 7:00 a.m. so she could get ready for work along with her family.

Even though Pasty, Peggy, Pauline, and Pamela were good witches, they still had to work outside of the house to maintain their household.

Paul always tried to help with keeping the manor clean and in good working order. Paul took care of the yard also. The reason Paul did all the things was he wanted to help the sisters as much as he can. They all work outside of the home, and Paul worked with Peggy at the club when he was scheduled to work. Everyone living in the manor always tried to keep everything nice and neat. So, after the sisters and the rest of the gang went to work, Paul was ready to order the P3 to help Peggy with the stock. He orbed to Peggy's office so just in case anyone was there, they would not see Paul orbed in. It didn't take long before he was ready to get started to work. He walked down the stairs to find that his boss Peggy's wife was behind the bar.

Peggy looked up and said, "There you are, Paul. I'm glad you're here. The stock truck just came in. The truck needs to be unloaded in a separate stock. Would you mind doing that for me, please?"

Paul says, "Is everything all right?"

Peggy says: Yes, I was just about what time he was in the year because the truck just got brought our stock for P3? I just wanted to make sure he can be here to put it away.

Peggy was getting P3 set up and ready for the night shift and their clients to come in and enjoy their self and relax. Paul went ahead and started to try putting a stop way in bringing the stock downstairs to the bar force Peggy to put the bar for spare. Once Paul was done putting away the stock, he had been notified by the elders to come see them. Paul walked where Peggy was and told her the elders just notified him that they need to see him. Paul says: I will be back.

Peggy says: All right, I'll see if the manor then.

Paul says: All right, I'll see you when I get back. I will manor how meet you there.

Paul walked back upstairs to Peggy's office, where Paul orbed to see the elders. The elders wanted Paul to start teaching at magic school, and he said: I would love to do this, but I need to talk it over with Peggy first. Will I draw a paycheck?

The elders say: Yes, you will because eventually the world's going to know about you guys.

Paul says: How is that possible? I understood that were not supposed to let we be known as white lighter to regular people and witches, even if were good witches were not supposed to let me know supposed to be a secret.

The elders said: Yes, that is as a now, very, very soon you guys you all will be none, and it will not be as bad as you think. I need you to go back to the girls and bring them to me. I need to see the sister all for you today as soon as possible Paul?

Paul says: I will bring them to you if I must bring in one of, I will bring them to you until you have all four of them in your eyesight.

John says: Thank you very much, Paul. I appreciate your willingness to do as we ask.

Paul says: I'll be back.

With that Paul orbed that to the manor. He arrived at the manor, and no one was home yet. Paul took the trash out, checked the mail and went upstairs to take a shower and change in the short and put his tennis shoes on. As he walked back downstairs going to the living room, the phone rang. Paul answered, and it was Peggy. Peggy says: I'll be home in the elder's name John about 30 minutes.

Paul says: When you to see, the elder John.

Peggy says: That's fine. Everybody should be on the my five today.

Paul says: Well, as each one comes home, I must orb them up to see Elder John. That is, all you four sisters.

Peggy says: I will let the rest of my sisters know what's going on.

Paul says: Thank you so much for helping me out with this.

Peggy says: No problem. You might have seen you need my help here and there wherever you need me.

Paul and Peggy hung up the phone Peggy when I will work Paul hung out until the everybody started coming home when the four sisters were up there with Elder John along with Paul Elder John explained everything to the Williams sisters that eventually the world would know they were all good witches they would also be looked at as if they were heroes but your magic still stands you only use your magic against evil demons you must never hurt innocent but you will always be known and she goes heroes for your good deeds for all of your good deeds. Peggy says: We don't want to be heroes, but we still want to be good witches, and I don't know if the public should know about us.

Elder John says, "Please don't worry. I promise you everything will be fine."

Meanwhile, everyone was at work, which gave spirit the opportunity to rummage through the Williams manor. The spirit entered the Williams manor from the bottom floor. She walked through the front door of the Williams manor. The spirit went from room to room on the bottom or looking and seeing what she could learn about the person that she wanted to take with her as has her companion. As the spirit, would complete each room on the bottom floor and she was content she had learned everything on the bottom floor that she could learn about Peggy. The spirit gently loaded up the stairs to the second floor of the Williams manor, making her rounds to every room on the second floor to learn more about Peggy. Finally making her way up to the attic where the book of shadows with their and the trap that Paul had set for anyone demon or spiritual, we get caught in a went here the book of shadows. The spirit went all over the attic, looking plundering do things studying just as hard as she could be learning everything possible there is to learn about Peggy. Once the spirit was satisfied and knew that she had completed her task only over with a fine-tooth comb of the Williams manor that spirit then evaporated disappeared.

Soon, Peggy realized it was close to noon, and she would have wanted to go home and have. Peggy's morning cashier came in and watched the bar, while Peggy and Paul went home to have lunch. As soon as cashier Cindy had the register counted out, she was ready watch over the club. Peggy decided it was time to go find Paul. She walked upstairs to the storage area where their storage room was. That is where she found Paul just finishing unloading and putting away all the stuff that came. Peggy says: Paul, let's go home and have lunch.

Paul says: Are you ready to go now? Peggy says: Yes.

Peggy walked over to where Paul was standing and took his hand. Paul and Peggy orbed to the manor. They landed in the kitchen, and Peggy went ahead and started fixing lunch so that they could have lunch together.

Now the spirit when she vanished out of the house and the manor, she went on to see if he can find George Mathis. George Mathis is the one who turned the spirit on to Peggy. The reason George Mathis did this was he was trying to break apart all the Williams sisters so that he can get them by themselves one at a time and try to destroy them. The spirit suddenly had a feeling or a suspicion that Peggy was close by, so she went back to the Williams manor, answering the Williams manor where the sunroom is where she quietly while she listens to Peggy in the kitchen getting lunch ready for her and her husband. Little did Peggy and Paul know that the spirit was closer than they thought. Peggy and Paul sat down at the table where they ate lunch totally table sat and drinks ready for them while they ate their lunch.

Soon, Peggy and Paul were done with their lunch; and while Peggy went upstairs to use the restroom to make sure that her makeup was okay, Paul cleaned up the kitchen and put everything away and took the trash out. The spirit was upstairs in the attic, away from everyone, but she can hear what their conversation was about. Once Peggy was done, she came back downstairs to see that Paul was sitting in the living room, waiting for her to go back to work. Paul got out walked over to Peggy to her hand, they are back to work. They landed in Peggy's office, which was locked so no one can enter. It made it safe for her and Paul to travel in and out of the restaurant when I have the with Peggy and her vehicle.

Pauline did work, but she was also in college. College classes were in the morning, so by afternoon, she goes to work at the *San Francisco Chronicle*. The *San Francisco Chronicle* has a love inquiry page, and that is what Pauline's job was—to take care of all the love needed. Pasty and Peggy was always on by five thirty every afternoon Monday through Friday. Pauline and Pamela were always home by six thirty every evening.

So, by seven o'clock every evening at the manor was when the Williams sisters and their family would eat dinner. Peggy was the one that did the cooking, so she also always made sure that dinner would be served no later than seven every evening. Paul was always home by five thirty. Mike would be home by six fifteen every evening. So, for a Peggy came home from work it was five thirty, and said after they arrived home, they notice the front door was unlocked and not shut all the way. Peggy instantly darted, freaking out and panicking, and it was Pasty that would calm Peggy down by talking. When Paul came home, the orbed and kitchen, so he walked to the cabinet took a glass out walked to the refrigerator, Paul opened the refrigerator took the tea out of the refrigerator, set the tea on the counter and took the lemon out. Paul went to the silverware drawer, got a sharp knife out, shut the drawer, and walked back over to where his glass iced tea pitcher and lemon were. Paul sliced some lemons and put the ice in his glass. He poured the tea and put the lemon back in the refrigerator and shut the door with a knife in her think and walked into the living room. He sat in the recliner and he turned the TV on. Paul saw the note that Peggy left him. He read the note, got up, and went back to the kitchen that you and put it in a colander, Paul walked outside and started the grill. Once the grill was started, he walked back into the house to season the chicken and to get out there, so it would be ready to go on the grill. Meanwhile, Pasty and Peggy came home from work. Pasty went upstairs to her room to get a shower and change to her home or sleeping clothes. Peggy walked outside where Paul was and said: I will take a shower and get comfortable. I will be back to start our dinner.

Paul says: Okay.

It wasn't long before Pasty and Peggy were back downstairs Peggy was in the kitchen making mashed potatoes, green salad, some garlic toast, and fresh tea. Pasty went into the living room where she sat down and out, I was watching TV watching the news. Pasty like to watch the news so she can catch up on what had happened during the day while she was at work. It wasn't long before Pauline and Pamela came home from work. They too went upstairs got a shower and went back downstairs in the living room where they sat down on the out and started watching TV. Soon after everyone was home and back downstairs, Peggy came in the living room and told Pasty, "Please go ahead and set the table."

Pasty got up walked in the kitchen, opened the cabinet at the plates out that glasses out brought everything to the table the dining room table and started setting the table back in the kitchen and got the napkins so that she sent the table in the dining room.

Peggy says, "Pamela, can you turn your notice at work?"

Pamela says, "Yes, I did, and he was not happy about it."

Peggy says, "What did your boss say?"

Pamela says, "My boss said he would accept my regular nation, but he really wasn't happy about it. He wished that I would reconsider and work for them, but it really does not matter what he wants or how he feels about it because I am going to be working for my sister to help her with her club."

Peggy says, "I am so glad to be home and know that you're going to be working at my club to help me."

Peggy then walked into the kitchen. Pasty and Pamela went into the kitchen, got the glasses with ice out, came back in the dining room, and sat around the table.

Peggy says: Everybody needs to the dining room and let's get ready to eat dinner. The whole game walked into the dining room, sat down at the table, and started passing the food around. Soon, everyone was eating and enjoying their meals when suddenly there was a knock at the door, something sounding like it was all in the attic. This was all happening at the same time.

Peggy says: I will answer the door.

Mike says: Paul and I will go upstairs to the attic he will down.

Pasty says: I'll answer the phone.

Pauline says: Pamela and I will stand right here and help if you need help.

Everybody went back to the dining room table and sat down and started eating again. Peggy says: That was a salesman at the door.

Pasty says: That was wrong number on the phone.

Paul and Mike are back into the dining room and said: Oh my god, you will not believe this.

Peggy says: What?

Paul says: We caught George Mathis in our trap in the attic.

Everybody jumped up from the table ran to Paul and started holding hands. The four Williams sisters were holding hands. Peggy took Paul hand, and they orbed to the attic. She froze George Mathis. Peggy then unfroze Cole's head and says: What on earth do you think you're doing, George Mathis? And before George Mathis disappeared. Everybody turned around and looked at each other like what happened where did he go. So, everybody held hands again. Peggy took Paul's hand, and they orbed back to the dining room where they all sat down and finished eating their supper. Once they were all done eating, Pamela and Pauline cleaned up the kitchen and dining room.

After Pamela and Pauline cleaned up the kitchen, everyone else was in the living room, watching television. That is when Pamela and Pauline went to the living room to be with the rest of the family. Mike was sitting next to Pasty. Pasty got off the couch and walked in to the kitchen and took the calendar off the wall and takes it into the living room. She sits down by Mike. Pasty looked at the calendar and said: We can get married in two months.

Mike says: That would be in June, right? Pasty says: Yes, the fifteenth, if that sounds all right with you.

Mike says: That sounds like a plan.

Pasty says: June 15, we will get married right here in the manor.

Mike says: It is a date.

Pamela orbed up to the attic and grabbed the spells for all the demons that were yet to come or at least ready for.

Pasty, Peggy, Pauline, and Pamela waited until the whirlwind started blowing as if the worst kind of evil you can imagine the manor. Once the whirlwind started, Pasty, Peggy, Pauline, Pamela felt the evil that had entered the manor.

Chapter 4

THE WAY THAT THEY FELT WAS SO COLD and pure evil—unadulterated, the kind that would make your body crawl. It was so evil. before of the Williams sisters stood there in the wake of the worst imaginable feeling they had ever felt before and believe me they knew evil this kind of evil never even dreamt in their wildest imagination. The Williams sisters said: four of them together evil and that below that which forms below no longer will you do well that takes you with the spell was the spell they needed to say. So once the apparition appeared of the evilest besides the source of all evil, the Williams sisters said that spell. Once the spell was said, an explosion happened not blowing up the house blowing out windows where the force of the way the whirlwind exploded and made all four of the Williams sisters unconscious, lying on their backyard.

The Williams sisters said: The spell was the charm.

Paul and Mike were at the magic school. The elders informed Paul that he needed to go down and revive the Williams sisters. He left Mike there to be safe. Paul orbed to the manor where he found his wife and three sisters all lying on their backyard unconscious. He revived all four of them and asked them: What on earth just happened?

Pasty says, "We set a spell to get rid of some evil Mike destroyed our house and through us outside in the backyard it tried to take us out, but we took it out instead. I would be waking up by you. Thank you very much. Please help us up."

Once the girls could be set up and, on their feet, they had Paul and told him thank you very much they appreciated his help.

Pasty says, "Is it safe to bring Mike back yet?"

Paul says, "I'm not sure when he orbs back to the elders and find out that you guys help, and I'll let you know when I find out. I'll be back."

Peggy says, "Okay, I guess we will be cleaning up the mess while you are gone."

Paul orbs to the elders to find out if the evil is done for now.

The elders say: Oh yes, you can bring Mike back to the manor, and everybody will be fine. Now we can move forward with our plans.

Soon Mike and Paul were home again. They continued to finish cooking the barbecue chicken. It was time for the barbecue sauce.

Peggy fixed the rest of the dinner. Pasty and Pauline set the table. Pamela came downstairs to help Pauline put the glasses with ice and him and bring the first tea out dining room table. Once they were all done, and Pamela and Pauline brought the food that Peggy put in bowls and placed it on the dining room table and I'll be able to sit down and eat as soon as the chicken was done. Soon Paul came in and got a flatter chicken on. Mike brought the chicken in the house. Paul turned off the grill and brought all the stuff back into the house so that it will be put away after dinner. Once Peggy put the chicken on the dining room table, everyone sat down to enjoy a wonderful meal that Pasty, Peggy, Pauline, Pamela, Paul, and Mike had fixed. Everyone enjoyed the meal. They had conversation about their day and what they planned for tonight. Once dinner was done, everybody got up. Pauline and Pamela cleaned the kitchen and dining room. While Pasty and Peggy, along with Paul and Mike, went into the living to watch some TV. Once the kitchen and the dining room were cleaned up, Pauline and Pamela walked in to the living room where the rest of the game was sitting down watching TV. They all started talking about different things that was going on. Mike said to Paul: Paul can I talk to you in private?

Paul says: Sure.

Paul got up and walked into the kitchen. Mike led the way. He says: I have the ring in my pocket. I want to ask Pasty to marry me.

Paul says: Good idea. Let me get the rest of the gang so that you and Pasty can be alone. Mike says: I appreciate that.

Mike was not aware that Paul, Peggy, Pauline, and Pamela are already in on this. Paul looked at Peggy. Peggy looked at Pauline and Pamela. They all got up and walked out of the living room, leaving Pasty and Mike alone. Paul and Peggy went to their room. Pauline and Pamela also went to their very own bedrooms, getting their clothes ready for work tomorrow. they had busy days coming up this week.

So, Paul and Mike searched the downstairs and was unable to find Pasty and Peggy. Paul says: maybe we should try looking upstairs.

Mike says: Good idea. That's a good plan. The up the stairs they both went Paul and Mike looking for their wives and girlfriends.

Once Mike and Paul were upstairs, the first thing Paul says: I will look in my room and Peggy's room, and you go looking in Pasty's room to see if you can find her.

Paul walked into Peggy's room where he found Peggy getting her clothes ready for work tomorrow. Monday was a busy workday, and they all the work on Mondays. Mike found Pasty in her room and close ready for work for tomorrow they had already gotten their showers, so they were in their jammies. Mike and Paul walked back in the hallway. Paul says: I found Peggy.

Mike says: I found Pasty.

Mike and Paul walked back downstairs to give the girls their privacy so that they can get ready for Monday. Mike and Paul went to the living room and sat down to watch TV. Pasty came downstairs and walked into the living room where Mike and Paul were watching TV. Paul says: We need to put candles out and get the Champaign on ice, and Peggy and I will make sure you and Pasty's bedroom are all set up for romance tonight.

Mike says: Thanks, man, I appreciate everything you are doing for Pasty and me.

Paul says: Listen, I happen to know for a fact that you truly love Pasty with all your heart, and you want to spend the rest of your lives together.

Mike says: Thank you for all the families help to be together.

Paul says: Besides I want you as my brother-in- law. Is that all right with you, Mike?

Mike says, "Yes, it is all right with me. I am going to play some of Pasty's favorite romantic music."

Paul says, "That is a great idea. See, that is why I like you. You are always thinking of a way to be helpful with romances." knew that Pasty had walked down stairs they all went into Pasty's room and made her room ready for romance.

Peggy broke off rose petals and placed them all over Pasty's bed, and there were candles placed all over the bedroom. Pauline turned back Pasty's bed, so it would be ready.

The by the time, probably Peggy, Pauline and Pamela came downstairs that was Paul signal to let Mike know that everything is all set. Paul was standing in the doorway of the living room, talking to Pasty and Mike. While Pasty was not looking, Paul winked at Mike. Mike knew that Pasty's room was ready, and tonight was going to be the night that he proposes to Pasty. Peggy, Pauline, Paul, and Pamela walk in the kitchen, got the drink, and went back upstairs to leave Pasty and Mike alone.

Mike lit the candle in the living room, and he turned on some nice romantic music that Pasty would love.

Mike opened the champagne bottle and poured two glasses of champagne. Mike went down on one knee and took her left hand and he said, "Pasty, you know I love you. You know I want to spend the rest of my life. Please give me the honor of becoming my wife."

Pasty says, "Oh my god! Yes, yes, yes, yes!"

Peggy, Pauline, Paul, and Pamela heard what Pasty said and ran in the living room to hug her.

Paul and Peggy both walked into the kitchen and grabbed some champagne glasses and brought them to the living room Mike court campaign in each glass Paul offered a toast for Mike and Pasty. Paul says: It's about going to you to tie the knot we have been wait and wait and wait for a long time for this to happen. May you always have a close to normal of life that you possibly can and may you both walking the throughout your lifetime commitment.

Mike says: Hear, hear! I'll drink to that.

They all had a sip of champagne. Pasty and Mike retired up to Pasty's bedroom, where the rest of the night romance would take place. Paul told Peggy, Pauline, and Pamela: Go upstairs to bed. I'll be a little bit off to clean up downstairs.

Peggy says: Thank you, honey. I really appreciate that.

The girls then retired to their rooms. Paul stayed downstairs to clean up the living room and put away everything, making sure the kitchen was clean and straight down the trash was out lights were out doors were locked windows was shut locked and the cat was outside.

While everyone was sleeping, the spirit that have been pursuing Peggy in her attic. And as she was loading along and checking things out triggered the alarm that Paul had set. The moment the alarm went off, the spirit disappeared. Paul jumped up and or to be immediately, to reset the alarm and see if what he had caught. Of course, there was nothing there, so Paul decided that he would set another trap for whoever this is. Paul had no idea that George Mathis had contacted the spirit and made a deal with her. George Mathis was casually watching invisible course what the spirit was looking for and about. Once Paul finished with checking things out in the attic and resetting the alarm and setting the other trap, he decided that he would Rest house to make sure that everything was fine. Once Paul had made his rounds the check all the windows and doors sure that everything was locked up and the Williams sisters would be safe and sound in their home.

Everybody was sleeping and resting, and they're all in a very deep sleep. It was now 7:00 a.m. You could hear Peggy's alarm going off. Peggy got up during the alarm and went to the bathroom to shower and get dressed for the day make up and all shoes was outside of the bedroom. When she was done getting ready for work, she made her way to the kitchen. By this time, Pasty's alarm had gone off. Pasty got up and took a shower and dressed for the day. She grabbed her shoes her purse and came downstairs.

Now Mike was a police officer and investigator who had to be at work by 7:00 a.m. He was up at 5:00 a.m. showered shaved ready for work leaving the house at 6:30 AM. Send it wasn't long Pauline and Pamela were up showered dressed for work downstairs in the kitchen having coffee with their sister. Everybody was ready for work.

Everyone had their breakfast, and off to work they went. Paul cleaned up the kitchen and made sure that all the trash was out. Paul then went to the attic to see if he'll see the spirit or anything out of place. Paul looked all over the attic, checking to make sure the alarm was set for all evil to be trapped. Once Paul was satisfied that everything was all right, he then orbed to the magic school for work.

While everyone was at work, the spirit that was doing George Mathis's bidding with such evil intent to cause such horrible devastation to the Williams sisters, and hurt the rest of the family with such loss. George had been lurking around the Williams manor, trying to figure a way to get the book of shadows out of the Williams manor to take it to the source of all evil. So far everything George tries does not work for him. The source of all evil was growing impatient with him to complete his job that was assigned to him—to kill the Williams sisters at all cost. The source pulled George Mathis down to him and says: George Mathis, you are to kill the Williams sisters at all cost, and if you can't do that, then at least cripple them where they are not the power of 3 or 4. George Mathis had sworn allegiance to the source many years ago, so of Paul had decided as he was orbing into the kitchen to get him something to drink that he would orb to the attic and check out the house before the girls arrived home.

Once Paul arrived home and got him a glass of tea to drink and as Paul was getting ready to orb to the attic, he heard a knock at the front door. Paul walked in to the foyer to the front door, and as he opened the door, he saw it was Mike. Paul says: Mike, you do not have to knock. You're staying here, and if you don't have a key, we will get you one.

Mike says: Yes, I know, and Pasty is getting her key back from Peggy. When they get home, I believe we will go and get me a key made after that.

Paul says: Cool, glad to hear that. I am headed up to the attic. You want to come along?

Mike says: Yes, I would like to help in protecting. Paul laughed and said: You're very funny.

Mike laughed too. Mike and Paul stepped back into the kitchen so that Mike could get him something to drink, and off to the attic they orbed. Paul had put his arm around Mike, so they could orb together, and once they arrived at the attic, Paul said: I am sorry. It is either my arm around you, or we must hold hands. Mike looks at Paul as if to say "Really?"

Mike says: Well, if that is the way you must do, that's okay.

Paul says: I can hold your hand if you rather.

Mike says: Well, if you don't tell anyone except for this family, I really don't care. It is up to you.

Mike held his hand out to Paul, and they shook hands. Mike and Paul were becoming close to each other as if they were brothers.

While Paul and Mike were in the attic, Peggy and Pasty went into the kitchen and made two glasses of tea to drink while they were on the way to their bedrooms so that they could get a quick shower and change into some shorts and a T-shirt to be more comfortable. As soon as Peggy was done, she grabbed her tea glass and headed downstairs so that she could go ahead and start dinner. Peggy was making spaghetti and meatballs with fresh garlic toast from the fresh bread she baked two nights ago. Meanwhile, Paul and Mike had completely checked the attic and found that a few things were out of place. Since they wanted to have the Williams sisters check it out, they did not touch a thing in there. As soon as Peggy had fixed her garlic toast and was getting ready to put it in the oven, Paul walked into the kitchen and said: We need to have a family meeting after dinner. Peggy jumped because she had her back turned from Paul, and, he startled Peggy. Peggy to come set the dinner almost dropped the garlic toast as she was getting ready to put it in the oven.

Peggy says, "Paul, is everything all right?"

Paul says, "Maybe! Or maybe not. Mike and I have somethings we want to show Pasty, so please set the dining room table. Dinner will be done soon." Paul says: sure.

Paul walks outside where Pasty is standing with Mike. Paul says, "Pasty, after dinner, we are having a family meeting because Mike and I discovered some evidence that shows that something or someone has been in the attic and possibly all over the manor."

Paul told Pasty that Peggy was ready for her to set the table in the dining room. Pasty walked into the kitchen to get everything she would need to set the table for dinner. Pauline and Pamela finally made it home from work, and they went upstairs and to take a shower and put on their shorts and T-shirts. As Pauline and Pamela were all done with changing their clothes and getting dressed, they came downstairs just in time for Pauline to put the ice in the glasses for tea to drink with their dinner. It was not long before it was time to eat. Peggy walked out of the kitchen and into the living room, and she told everyone it was time for dinner. Everyone got up from their seat in the living room and started walking to the dining room, and as each one of them sat down at the table to get ready to eat, Paul says: Hopefully, we will get to enjoy our meal that my sweet wife prepared.

Peggy says: Yes, let's hope so. My food always tastes better when it is fresh and hot.

Pasty, Pauline, Pamela, Mike, and Paul says: Peggy, you are so right.

Everyone could enjoy their meal. Once the meal was finished, they all got up from the table, and Pamela and Pauline started cleaning up the dining room and the kitchen. The rest of the gang went back into the living room except for Pasty. She had received a letter back from her cousin, and he has agreed to move back to California to live with his three sons, one daughter, and his wife.

Pasty was so excited that she heard from her cousin that she ran downstairs to tell the rest of the gang what James had said in the letter. James told Pasty: If you can find a place for my family and I to purchase, we will be happy to move back to San Francisco, California.

James even told Pasty that some very strange things had been going on with their family. James told Pasty: I cannot wait to see you so that I can show and tell you what has been going on.

Once Pasty had read the entire letter to the family, they all were so excited to know that James and his family were moving back. Pasty decided that on her lunch break, she would call a real estate company and see what she could find out for James. Pasty will call James and tell him what she can do for him.

While everyone was discussing about James, the alarm in the attic went off. Everyone jumped up and held hands as Paul orbed everyone up to the attic. Once they were all in the attic, Pauline saw the spirit in the trap. Pauline took one of the crystals and said this to the spirit: Spirit what are you doing here?

The spirit turned and looked at Holly and held out her hand and said: Come with me, Holly says never.

Holly says: I will never go with you. I don't care what you want. The answer is no.

The spirit held her head down, and she started spinning around until she exploded. When the spirit exploded, it made a great big mess out of the attic. Holly says: Oh, great, now we get to clean up the attic.

Mike says: This is so creepy and very strange.

Pauline says: Just look at this mess. This is so wrong. Demons and spirits make such a mess when they die.

Then out of nowhere, George Mathis appears and says: Pauline, you will be my wife.

Pauline says: Only when Hell freezes over will that take place.

Pauline then turn her back on George, and he vanished into thin air.

Pauline says: That man will never leave me alone.

Chapter 5

It was eight thirty on a beautiful Saturday. The birds were chirping because it was a spring day. Peggy was up and on her way to the kitchen to make coffee for her family. She had also taken out some plates for everyone because she made crescent rolls, scrambled eggs, and bacon. Pasty came walking down the stairs. As she was almost to the bottom of the stairs, Pauline came walking down. Pasty stopped at the bottom of the stairs and waited for Pauline, as they were walking to the kitchen Rose started down the stairs. Soon, everyone was downstairs and, in the kitchen, enjoying their coffee and breakfast. Peggy says: We should all make plans and spend the day doing something together.

Pasty says: The only thing I want to do is to study about our powers so that we can be better prepared in case we ever get a chance to kill the source of all evil.

Rose says: That is a good idea.

So as soon as breakfast was done, Paul and Mike went off, so the girls would have the house to themselves. Peggy and the rest of the gang knew if they needed Paul, all they had to do was call his name.

So, the four sisters study books on their powers. While they were studying, George Mathis had brought the spirit back to chase after Peggy. Pasty says: Peggy, do you think that spirit is gone for good?

Peggy says: I hope so. She sure does creep me out. I never have figured out why she wants me all to herself.

Pasty says: I don't know, but just in case, I would prefer you not to be alone I have a sneaky feeling that she is not gone at all.

Pauline says: If George Mathis has anything to do with it, she is still hanging out with him.

Soon, the girls had decided they had studied enough, and Paul and Mike came home. Peggy had already taken out the chicken, so they could have it for dinner. Suddenly, there was a strange noise coming from the attic. Mike says: What the heck was that?

Paul says: It sounds like the alarm in the attic is going off.

Mike says: Okay, we cannot leave the sisters down here alone just in case someone might be downstairs.

Paul says, "We will all orb upstairs to the attic, but first, we can check downstairs first." Everyone went through each room downstairs. Once they were satisfied that there was no one or no demons downstairs, Paul says, "Peggy, Pasty, Pauline, and Rose, please hold hands. Mike, come stand between Peggy and Pasty so we can orb up to the attic."

Once everyone was all holding hands, Paul walked over to Peggy and took her hand. As soon as Paul took Peggy's hand, they all orbed up to the attic. Once they all arrived in the attic, Rose walked over to the trap and lifted eon of the crystals.

Pasty says, "Why are you here in our attic? What is your problem?"

The spirit says, "I need Holly to come with me."

Peggy says, "That is never going to happen. I don't want to be with you."

The spirit says, "I need you to come with me." Peggy says, "Never."

Peggy tried to freeze the spirit, and just then, George Mathis said, "I will never stop until Pauline is my wife."

Pauline says, "Never going to happen, Cole. You are pure evil, and you will never marry me. You are the source of all evil, and I will not be your queen ever."

Just then, George and the spirit vanished. Rose puts the crystal back, and it resets the trap.

Paul says, "Everyone joins hands, so we can orb back downstairs."

Everyone joined hands, and they all orbed back downstairs. Peggy went to the kitchen to make a fresh pitcher of tea, so they would be able to have something to drink for the afternoon. Paul and Mike went outside to start the grill. Pasty walked into the kitchen and decided she wanted to make a green salad to go with the rest of the dinner. Peggy says: Thank you so much, sisters, for your help with our dinner.

Pasty went ahead and set the dining room table for dinner. Pauline and Pamela were in the living room, talking about the spirit that has been chasing after Peggy. Pamela told Pauline: Together we can take care of the spirit.

Paul picked up the container that Peggy had put the chicken in, and he took it outside and put it on the grill. Pasty walked upstairs to her room.

Pamela says: Pauline, we need to have a private meeting with Peggy about the wedding shower we are planning for Pasty's wedding.

Pauline says: How are we going to do that? Pauline says: Pasty hates surprise parties.

Pamela says: Not a problem, we can do the private meeting when we are away from home and Pasty is at work. That way we can keep it as a surprise.

Pauline says: That is a good idea.

Pasty came walking back downstairs and went into the sunroom, so she could reread her letter she had from her cousin Jack. Pasty had decided that she would go Monday to talk to a realtor and see if she would be able to get a house for her cousin to live in and have his family with him. Pasty sat in a comfortable chair in the sunroom and started writing a letter to her cousin. Paul came into the manor to get the barbecue sauce for the chicken and told Peggy the chicken will be done in about ten minutes. Peggy says: Oh, okay, I will go ahead and get the rest of the food in bowls, and I will have Pamela help me.

Paul says, "That sounds good."

Peggy walked in to the living room and says, "Pamela, would you come help me in the kitchen, please?"

Pamela says, "Sure, no problem." Pamela helped Peggy in the kitchen, and it was not long before Pauline came into the kitchen to ask if she could help.

Peggy says, "Yes, you can go open the French doors so that Paul and Mike can bring the chicken in. Once you have done that, find Pasty and tell her it is time to eat."

Pauline opened the doors for Paul and Mike, and then she went into the sunroom and told Pasty to come eat.

Pasty says, "Okay, I am on my way."

Once everyone was at the table, they all started passing the food around, and they all enjoyed their meal. Pasty, Peggy, Pauline, and Pamela along with Paul and Mike loved to eat as a family. They all knew how much it meant to Peggy to do things as a family, and they would always love to spend family time together.

Once dinner was done, Pauline and Pamela cleaned up the dining room and the kitchen while everyone else went their separate ways. Peggy and Paul went into the living room, and Pasty and Mike went into the sunroom. Peggy and Paul were watching television, and Pasty and Mike were just sitting in the sunroom, having a nice chat about their wedding. It took Pauline and Pamela about thirty minutes to get everything done in the dining room and kitchen. Once they were done, they both had dates. Pauline and Carl Manning were on their way to see a movie. Pamela and Jack Marble was on their ways to the mall to have something to do. Paul got up and says: I think I am ready for bed. What about you, Peggy?

Peggy says: Yes, that sound like a very good idea.

Paul and Peggy went upstairs to their bedroom, and Peggy picked out the outfit that she was going to wear to church. She set her alarm to go off at seven thirty in the morning. It was not long before Pasty and Mike headed up to bed. Pasty picked out her outfit she was going to wear for church in the morning. Pasty set her alarm for 7:15 a.m.

It was about 11:00 p.m., and that was when Pauline and Carl Manning came home from the movies, and they went straight to bed. Pauline picked out her outfit for church and set her clock for 7:30 a.m. It was not long after that Pamela and Jack Marble came home. Jack Marble dropped off Pamela at home, and he went back to his apartment. Carl Manning also left and went back to the magic school where he lived.

Pamela made sure all the doors were locked, and then she went to bed.

Everyone was sound asleep in the manor. Meanwhile, George Mathis was lurking around in the manor. He was still trying to take the book of shadows out of the manor and as George tried to take the book of shadows out the front door when the book of shadows hit the floor and made a loud noise that woke everyone in the house up. Paul and Peggy both jumped out of bed and went running into to the foyer to see what the noise was. It was not long before everyone was up and at the front door to see what had happened. Pasty saw the book of shadows lying by the front door. This concerned Pasty. Pasty says, "Hey, look right by the front door. The book of shadows is there."

Peggy says, "Why is the book of shadows downstairs and not in the attic where it belongs?"

Pamela says, "That is a very good question."

Paul says, "It looks as if someone was trying to take it out of the manor."

Peggy says, "Who would do that?"

Pauline says, "Let me see if I can call a premonition."

Pauline walks over to the book of shadows and had a premonition. She saw George Mathis, the district attorney in the manor, trying to steal the book of shadows.

Pasty says, "I knew he was no good. He is evil through and through."

Pauline says, "Yes, he is, and he will not stop until I get married."

Everyone looked around the manor and put the book of shadows back in the attic, and they all went back to bed.

Pasty's alarm went off, and she got up, took a shower, got dressed, put her makeup on, and then she fixed her hair. Peggy was up and showered, and she was ready for church. Peggy was downstairs, and she had breakfast fixed and the coffee made for her family. She's ready for her whole family to come and eat and drink coffee so they all could go to church.

Then everyone was on their way to church. It did not take long for all them to arrive. Once they all arrived and went inside the church, they found a place to sit. Once church was over, all the Williams family loaded up their cars, and home they went.

Soon they all arrived home, and they all went upstairs and changed their clothes. Paul and Mike went into the kitchen and put together everything they needed so that they could go to the park to have a family picnic. Paul and Mike loaded up their cars for the picnic. Pauline was waiting on Carl Manning to arrive. Jack Marble arrived at the Williams manor. Pamela had their picnic ready for them. Each couple made a picnic basket for their mate. Once all the picnic baskets were loaded up in each one of the Williams sisters' car, they all loaded up and took off for the park. Now the girls were very excited because the family would be able to enjoy some family time together. As they all are sitting at their blankets for the picnic and eating, Pasty and Mike are talking about their plans for their wedding. Pasty has been planning her wedding since she was dating Mike when they were in high school. She knows exactly what king of wedding she wants. It was getting late, and Pasty, Mike, Peggy, Paul, Pauline, Carl Manning, Pamela, and Jack Marble were ready to load up their cars and head back to the manor. That is exactly what they did. Once they arrived back to the manor, Jack Marble dropped Pamela off and went home. Pasty and Mike brought their basket to the kitchen and put all their picnic food that was left over into the fridge. Then they put their picnic basket into the laundry room on the shelf that they use for all their picnic blankets and baskets.

Peggy went upstairs and took a shower, while Paul put their picnic stuff away. Once Paul was done, he went upstairs to get a shower. Pauline and Carl Manning said goodnight at the front door of the manor. Once Carl Manning left, Pauline went upstairs and took a shower. It was not long before Pamela was upstairs in her room, and she had also taken her shower. Once everyone was showered and, in their jammies, they all came downstairs to enjoy a few minutes of relaxing in the living room. Peggy says: Good night, everyone. I need sleep.

It was not long before the rest of the gang were heading upstairs to their rooms to get a long- awaited rest. Peggy set her clock so that she would be able to get up and go to work. Pasty had her clock for 7:00 a.m. Mike set his for 5:00 a.m. Pauline, and Pamela also set the alarms for 7:00 a.m. Everyone had to work on Monday. Paul set his alarm for 7:30 a.m., and he always came downstairs right after Peggy and the rest of the sister were just leaving for work.

Paul loved it because he was downstairs just as all the sisters were leaving so that he could give his wife a kiss before she left for work. Then Paul would clean up the kitchen while he was having him some coffee, and he would have him some breakfast that his wife made for him. Then Paul would finish cleaning up the kitchen, including taking the garbage out. Paul would go upstairs to his room and take a shower and get ready to go to magic school. Paul was done with making sure the kitchen was cleaned, and he was ready for work and orbed to magic school.

George Mathis was making plans on how he could get rid of the Williams sisters. He was planning on kidnapping Pauline so that he could make her marry him. George called a meeting with all his best demons so that he could assign certain demons to keep a watch out on the Williams sisters. Now George knew that it would not be easy to kidnap Pauline because most of the time, she was not alone. Usually, Pauline had one or more of her sisters with her. George did not like any of the Williams sisters excepted for Pauline. Pauline was always afraid that something would happen to her, and she would end up leaving her family. All the Williams sisters were worried that something would happen to one of them, if not all of them, and they would not be around anymore. Peggy was always worried that Paul would be alone to raise their children. That was something that Peggy just could not handle. Peggy, Pasty, Pauline, and Pamela decided that since Pasty had been brought back to life and no one knew that time had been reset to when Mike and Pasty had died, and they changed their future for the better at least for now. Everyone in the family was safe as far as they all knew. The Williams sisters knew they would always have to fight the evil demons on this planet, and they also knew that in the end that it would be for all mankind.

It was almost time for Pasty and Peggy to come home from work. Paul was getting ready to orb home himself when the Elder John came over and started talking to Paul. Elder John says: I need you to bring your family here so that I can give them some news.

Paul says: All right, but you will have to wait until everyone is home from work.

Elder John says: How about after dinner?

Paul says: No problem. We will see you after dinner.

Paul orbed home to the manor.

Once Paul arrived home, he started seasoning the steak that Peggy had picked out that morning for dinner. Mike came home from work, and he walked outside where the grill is in the backyard. He started setting up the grill for dinner. Peggy and Pasty arrived at the manor. Peggy went to the kitchen and started wrapping potatoes in tinfoil to go on the grill. Pasty went into the kitchen and started putting a green salad together. Peggy started making a pot of fresh tea for dinner. About thirty minutes later, Pauline and Pamela came home from work. They went upstairs to take a shower and change to regular street clothes. They came back downstairs to help set the dining room table.

Meanwhile, the spirit that have been floating around keep an eye on Peggy was up in the attic with George Mathis. George was telling the spirit: Don't give up. We will get Peggy to go with you.

The spirit says to George: How do you know that she will go with me?

George says: I have a plan on how that would work out.

The spirit says: Explain yourself. I don't understand.

George said: We're going to kidnap her. We're going kidnap Peggy and were, but I'm take her to a state placed underground. I am working on that as we speak. I have I certain demons to set up a Cave area that will be away from anyone else, it will have all the comforts of a home. As a matter of fact, it will be like the Williams manor. It will have running water, electricity, and food in the refrigerator. Holly will have everything she will possibly need to survive underground until we are able to convince her to go with you on a permanent basis.

George told the spirit not to worry. He would take care of everything. The spirit vanished along with George. They returned to the underground.

Peggy had wrapped all the potatoes so that they could be put on the grill. Peggy placed the potatoes on a cookie sheet so that Paul or Mike could carry them out to the grill. Paul walked in the kitchen and picked up the steaks and the potatoes and brought them outside. He set them on the table next to the grill. Mike had article in the grill and got started. As matter of fact, the grill was almost ready to start cooking.

Pauline and Pamela went into the kitchen and got everything they needed to set the dining table. Pauline also made sure there was plenty of ice to go into the glasses so that they would have iced tea for their dinner. Pasty had made a beautiful pie for dessert. Peggy made sure that they had ice cream to go with the pie.

It didn't take long for dinner to be done as Paul was walking into the house, burning out with him the steaks and baked potatoes. Pasty had set all the food on the table in the dining room so that everyone can enjoy their dinner. Just about that time, Peggy was ready to tell everyone the company Carl Manning orbed in to the dining room. Pauline brought out another plate, silverware, and a glass so that Carl Manning could have dinner with the family. Peggy told everyone to eat. As everyone was coming to the table, out of nowhere, the spirit showed up.

The spirit says to Peggy, "Please come with me. I promise I will not hurt you."

Peggy looks at the spirit and says, "No, I will not go with you now nor will like it would you ever."

The spirit let out this gosh-awful scream that make everybody's head hurt. As the spirit was doing this gosh-awful scream, it disappears.

Pasty says, "Why does the spirit keeps popping in and says that Peggy go with her?"

Paul says, "I know, but we need to help want to talk to us all of us."

Pasty, Peggy, Pauline, Pamela, Paul, Mike, and Carl Manning sit down and eat their dinner.

Pasty says, "After we eat our dinner, we need to have a family meeting, or we go see the elders."

Paul says, "That is a very good idea."

All the Williams sisters, along with the rest of the gang, eat their dinner and enjoy it.

As soon as everyone was done eating, Pasty, Pauline, and Pamela clean off the dinner table and the kitchen. The rest of the gang went into the living room and waited patiently so that when they can have their family before, they went elders. What everyone was in the living room, Paul says: We will have to plan on how to deal with the spirit later.

Pasty says: Paul, do you have a plan on your mind? Paul says: As a matter of fact, I sure do.

Chapter 6

Peggy says: Everybody stand up and join hands.

Everybody stood up the joint hands and Peggy held Paul can and it orbed up to the elders. Now everybody was up to where the elders are, the elders proceed to tell all the Williams sisters and their family that this spirit is very evil and can-do bodily harm to Peggy. Elder John says: We're not sure exactly what evil. She has her powers she has or if she can be turned in the good were not sure what we do need your help.

Peggy says: How can I help?

Elder John says: If you should be kidnapped, don't let it play out. We will help your sisters find you. We will allow Paul to be able to go underground if we need to. This is a good way to catch whoever is out to be behind you, and I have a feeling that George Mathis, the district attorney, is the one that is behind some of the evil that's going on.

Pauline says: I hope one day George Mathis goes away.

Elder John says: Yes, he will, but that's for another date. And another time. We don't have time for that today.

Pauline says: I understand, Elder John. I don't am I just want him gone.

Elder John says: I hope you ladies have a good evening, and we'll talk again real soon.

Peggy says: Everybody needs to join hands again.

Peggy reached over and held Paul's hand and then orbed back to the manor. By this time, it was late at night, and everybody was tired, so they all went upstairs to go to bed. Pasty, Pauline, and Pamela all told Peggy they loved her very much having her as their sister.

It was a beautiful Saturday morning. Dawn was breaking, and all through the Williams manor was the peaceful sound of sleep? The Williamses have been so busy with life and their powers and dealing with all the demons it seemed like there was never time to take good care of themselves. It seemed like they were always fighting demons, and no matter how hard they tried, they never took the time to take good care of themselves. The Williams sisters were in desperate need of rest and relaxation. Peggy took it upon herself weeks ago to set up an appointment with a spa so that the girls could relax and rest. She was the only one that knew about the appointment, what she was up and getting dress for the day she decided when she went downstairs to make coffee, she would tell everyone. Peggy got dressed went downstairs make coffee and breakfast for her family. Peggy set the table in the dining room so that everyone would enjoy their breakfast in peace. Once everybody was seated at the dining room table, they all could enjoy their breakfast with their coffee. Peggy says: Pasty, Pauline, and Pamela, we are all going to the spa today.

Pasty says: I like the way you think, Sister.

Pauline says: Peggy is always looking out for our best interest and health.

Peggy says: Well, if I don't, you guys wont.

Paul says: Cool. Mike, you and I can go shopping around at the stores.

Mike says: Yes, we can, and we can also see the car auctions.

Paul says: That is a good idea a very good one.

Once everyone was done eating, Pauline and Pamela cleaned up and the kitchen. Paul and Mike had left to go out to do guy stuff.

Since Pasty, Peggy, Pauline, and Pamela were dressed for the day, they all loaded up in their vehicles to go to the spa. It would be a half day at the spa. Once they were all through, Pasty, Peggy, Pauline, and Pamela decided it was time to go shopping. It was noontime, and they were hungry for lunch. They stopped at a restaurant and ordered lunch. They ordered a salad and a glass of tea. These four sisters enjoyed spending time 101 with each other. They also enjoyed spending time as sisters just hanging out doing girl thing. Pasty, Peggy, and Pauline enjoyed spending time with their new sister Pamela to get to know her. Paul was very happy to have Mike back in the family. Paul and Mike were good friends before they died and were brought back. As Paul and Mike were getting into the car, Paul said: I am so glad, Mike, you are back with us. I always like it when you and we could do things together.

Mike says: Thank you, Paul, I appreciate. I always consider you a good friend too. As a matter of fact, I was hoping you would be my brother-in-law.

Paul says: That's exactly what I was hoping for too.

After the girls were done at the spa and having lunch, they all decided it was time to go home and enjoy some quiet time. They waited for Paul and Mike to get back home to the manor. Once Pasty, Peggy, Pauline, and Pamela arrived back to the manor, they decided to study their powers. The Williams sisters always believed in being prepared. That included being prepared with their powers. After they studied for a couple hours, Peggy got up and went downstairs to the kitchen to check out that Paul had already taken out for dinner and she seasoned it. Peggy put it in the oven to bake.

It wasn't long after that Paul and Mike came home. Paul and Mike went to the sunroom and sat down and continued the conversation about the truck they want to get. Paul had already saved the money to buy him an old fixer-upper truck. Mike already had the money to, but Mike wanted to make sure that it would be okay with Pasty.

Mike got up, walked out of the sunroom, went into the dining room, and found Pasty there and asked her what she thought about the truck that he wanted to get. Mike had a picture of the truck that he wanted to get. Mike showed Pasty the picture of the truck that he wanted to get.

Pasty says, "I love it. Please go ahead and get the truck. That would be great."

Mike says, "Thank you so much for letting me get the truck."

Pasty says, "You're quite welcome, Mike."

Mike says, "Thank you very much. I appreciate your help." Pasty and Mike went into the automobile dealership and bought Mike's truck. Mike says, "Pasty, you drive your car, and I will drive my car back to the manor."

Pasty says, "Sounds good to me. I'll meet you back in the manor."

Pasty got into her car, cranked it up, and put her seatbelt on close your door to put it in drive and down the road she went heading back to the Williams manor. Mike got in his truck, shut the door, cranked it up, put the seat belt on, and drove to the manor.

Meanwhile, Paul orbs home. Paul had ordered into the kitchen where Peggy was. Paul says, "Mike just bought him a pickup truck. I want you and to take a ride to the car dealership so that I can show you the pickup truck that I want."

Peggy says, "That sounds good to me. Let's plan to do it soon."

It wasn't long before Mike and Pasty hold up in the driveway to the manor. Soon, Mike and Pasty walked into the house. They headed straight to the kitchen to get a new drink and hope that they find Peggy. Peggy and Paul were coming out of the kitchen, as Pasty and Mike was walking into the kitchen. Pasty says: Peggy, hang on a minute. I want to get to a glass of tea. You and I on the front porch so that I can show you Mike's new truck.

Peggy says: Sounds good. Can't wait. Here, let me grab me a glass of tea too.

Pasty says: Come on, Peggy, let's go outside so I can show you Mike's truck.

Peggy says: Let's go, I'm ready.

Pasty and Peggy walked out the front door of the manor and down the steps to the driveway. Pasty showed Peggy Mike's truck. Peggy says: Is this the kind of truck that Paul wants?

Pasty says, "Yes, but he wants an older truck, one that he can work on."

Peggy says, "That sounds good to me."

Peggy walked into the kitchen and started cooking dinner. Pasty walked in the kitchen and says, "Peggy, tomorrow would be a good day to go look at the truck that Paul wants. We can do this after work."

Peggy says, "I agree. Let's do it."

Pauline walks in the kitchen walks over to the refrigerator gets her, Pauline says: What are we talking about?

Peggy says: Here's your glass and tea. We're talking about Pasty and me going to the car dealership for the truck that Paul wants.

Pauline said: Thank you. That is so cool. Are you going to let Paul get it?

Peggy says: I'm really worried about letting him do it.

Pauline says: Peggy, you know that Paul will be thrilled.

Peggy smiled and said: Good. I live to make my man happy.

Pasty, Peggy, Pauline, and Pamela started laughing at what Peggy had said. Paul and Mike walked into the kitchen where Pasty, Peggy, Pauline, and Pamela was laughing. Paul says: What is so funny?

Pasty says: You would not understand, so don't worry about it.

Paul and Mike looked at each other and smiled and said: Mike and I are ready to cook the chicken on the grill.

Peggy says: I'm already for you all. Here, Mike, take this out with you so you can use this sheet pan to put the chicken on once it's done.

Paul and Mike took the bowl with the chicken and the sheet pan along with the big fork, so they would have it to use for the chicken.

Meanwhile, the girls made fresh tea and green salad, cupcakes for desserts, and mashed potatoes. Peggy had already made homemade rolls earlier. While everybody was waiting on chicken, the four girls went into the living room. It took about thirty minutes for the chicken to cook. As soon as Paul and Mike brought the chicken into the house, everybody went to the dining room table and sat down and started picking the plates and started fixing their plates and started eating. The Williams sisters, along with Paul and Mike, enjoyed their dinner. As they all were sitting at the dinner table and eating, they all were enjoying conversation about one another's day at work. As their dinner was winding down and everyone was full, each one would get up from the table and go into separate room. Peggy and Pasty walked into the sunroom. Pamela and Pauline started cleaning up the kitchen and dining room. Paul and Mike walked out to the backyard, so they could clean up the barbecue area and make sure everything was put where it was supposed to be. Soon as Mike was done, he walked back into the kitchen and took out all the garbage so that they would not have a stinking home. While Pasty and Peggy was in the sunroom, they were talking about Pasty's upcoming wedding to Mike. Pasty was getting more excited every day. She still could not believe that Mike and she were getting married. Pasty walked upstairs to get the magazines that she had been looking at for ideas for her wedding. She brought the magazines downstairs and took them back to the sunroom where Peggy was waiting for her. Pasty and Peggy both liked the same things, so that is why Pasty wanted to share her thoughts with Peggy before Pasty made her final decision for her wedding.

Mike and Paul were still outside when Pamela and Pauline finished cleaning the kitchen and dining room. Pamela and Pauline went upstairs and were talking about the evil that had been going on a lot since Pasty and Mike was brought back. Pamela was concerned that the evil George Mathis would cause Pauline such heartache. Pamela was trying her hardest to get really close to all her sisters, but she seemed to be getting closer to Pauline. Finally, all the Williams sisters and Paul and Mike were all in the living room watching television. As everyone was in engrossed in a movie they were watching, there was a sudden crash as if something or someone was breaking the manor. Pasty, Peggy, Pauline, Pamela, Paul, and Mike all jumped and said: Oh, my goodness, what was that?

They all jumped up out of their seats and went running out the front door of the manor, and as they ran out, they all turned around to look at the manor. Mike says: Where is the roof over the bedrooms of the manor?

Paul looked and said: Oh my god, what on earth is going on?

Pasty and Peggy looked at each other in disbelief at what they saw. Pauline says: Great, now someone is stealing the roof of our home. What is wrong with this picture?

Pasty says: I have no idea! Paul, you need to orb to the elders, so you might be able to find out what is going on.

Paul says: Pasty, that is a very good idea.

So, Paul orbed to the elders. Then Mike noticed that the roof was back on the manor over the bedrooms. Mike says: I don't understand how or why this is happening.

Pasty says: It is magical and very evil, I am sure.

Mike says: Then that is the Williams sisters' job and department, right?

Pasty says: Yes, you are right, Mike.

Pasty smiled at Mike, and Mike smiled back at Pasty. Those two were head over hills in love with each other, just like Paul and Peggy. Peggy new that Paul was her soulmate. Just like Pasty knew that Mike was the only man for her. It takes a very special bond between a man and a woman to know that they are soulmates. Pasty and Peggy knew that they had their soulmates in hand, and they never had intentions of letting their men go. Pasty, along with Peggy, felt they had a duty to protect their loves. They knew firsthand from Nancy and James how love can be broken. Pasty and Peggy made a promise not only to themselves, but they also made a promise to each other that if they found their soulmate, they would never let him go.

After everyone was ready for bed, Pasty turned off the television; and everyone, except for Paul and Mike, went upstairs. Paul and Mike straightened up the living room and made sure the windows were shut and locked. As they were walking out of the living room, they turned out the lights. Paul and Mike went through the whole house, making sure everything was locked up and safe for their family. Once Paul and Mike were done with every room including the attic, they both decided it was time for bed.

The night was still and quiet. It was almost as if peace was settling in. Outside there was a gentle rain with a gentle breeze blowing. This was good sleeping weather and peaceful dreams. That is what everyone had—peaceful dreams. This went on all through the night, but evil was not resting. Evil was making plans on how to hurt the Williams sisters. George Mathis was planning on stealing Peggy from her sisters. George knew that if Peggy was down where evil lurked, she would not be able to use her powers. Or that is what George thought.

After the rain stopped, it was time for Peggy to get up, shower, and get dressed for work. Peggy was so glad that today was Friday. After Peggy was ready for work, she went downstairs to the kitchen to get everything set up for her family for breakfast. Pasty soon was up and getting herself ready for work. Paul was still sleeping. Pauline and Pamela were up and getting ready for work. Soon, everyone, except for Paul, was downstairs enjoy their coffee and cereal for breakfast. Paul came walking down the stairs and headed to the kitchen where he finds Pasty, Pauline, and Pamela getting ready to leave for work. Peggy was clearing the dishes off the kitchen table when Paul walked into the kitchen. He walked over to his wife and gave her a kiss. Paul says: I will clean this up, so you can go on to work.

Peggy says: Oh, thank you so much for helping your wife.

Paul says: That is my job.

Peggy gave Paul a kiss and a hug and out the door she went on her way to work. Paul poured himself a cup of coffee, sat down at the kitchen table, and fixed a bowl of cereal. Once Paul was done, he cleaned up the kitchen made sure the garbage was not ready to be taken out, and then he orbed upstairs took a shower and left for work.

It was around one o'clock in the afternoon when George let himself into the manor. He walked all over the manor. He made his way to Peggy's bedroom so that he could make sure that Peggy could have the exact same things in the manor in the manor where evil lived. George wanted everything to look and feel like the manor so that Peggy would at least be able to be comfortable. He had everything planned so that Peggy would even be able to go to her restaurant, and maybe she would not be so suspicions. It just wasn't Peggy whom George wanted, but he wanted all the Williams sisters and this manor kept. The only thing was they would not have their powers. George had everything planned so that it would happen in the middle of the night when everyone was sleeping. Paul and Mike would be separated from their family.

George kept his secret plans to himself. As a matter of fact, George did not even tell his closest demons that worked for him. George was thinking seriously about making the Williams sisters living in another plane. That way, they would not suspect anything right off, and George even thought about letter their powers work for them. He was even thinking about letting Paul and Mike be with the sisters on this different plane. Mike could still be a policeman, and Paul would not even know that they were living on a different plane. George had plenty of time. It was planned to take place after Pasty and Mike's wedding.

George happened to notice what time it was, and he left the manor. George knew that the Williams sisters would be home from work very soon. As a matter of fact, they all were on their way home from work. The Williams sisters were glad they did not have to work on Saturday. That meant they would be able to do some family things together.

The Williams sisters were all about family. Even though Peggy and Paul already had two children, Jonathan and Heterotherm, Peggy still enjoyed having all her sisters with her and spending time together.

Peggy and Pasty arrived at the manor first. As they parked their cars, they were giggling because Pasty was pulling into her parking spot in the driveway and Peggy pulled in right behind Pasty. Peggy and Pasty were so happy to be home from work. They walked up to the front door, and Peggy noticed her flowers that was planted by Paul about three weeks ago. They had blooms all over them. Peggy and Pasty and the rest of the sisters all loved to have fresh flowers in the manor.

Chapter 7

Why Won't George Stop

It was a Friday evening. Pasty and Peggy has just arrived at the manor. As Pasty and Peggy were walking into the manor, suddenly, the manor disappeared. It seemed as if the manor had vanished into thin air, but the manor was still there. They just could not see it. Pasty starts calling for Paul. Pasty says: Paul! Paul!

Paul appeared outside of the manor and says: What is wrong, Pasty?

Pasty says: Paul, do you notice anything different?

Paul says: Yes, where is the manor at? Peggy says: That is a good question.

Pasty says: We just arrived home, and this is what we found.

No sooner than Pasty said that, the manor reappeared.

Paul says, "This is very strange."

Pasty says, "You are telling us that? Paul, we need you to go inside the manor and make sure everything is all right."

Peggy says, "After you do that, please orb up the elders and see if you can please find out just what is going on."

Paul says, "I can do that."

Paul walked into the manor and checked everything out, and then he walked to the front door and opened it and told the sisters: It is safe. Come on in the manor. This is just too weird. Maybe you girls should go with me. At least that way I would know that you both are safe.

Pasty says: That is a great idea. Paul says: Thank you.

Peggy took Pasty's hand, and then Peggy took Paul's hand, and they all orbed up to the elders. John walked over to Paul and says: Boy, am I glad to see you.

Paul says: ya really what is going on?

John says: You are not going to believe this, but George Mathis is up to his old tricks. The Williams sisters are in big danger. George has no intentions of stopping until he makes Pauline fall in love with him and agrees to be his wife?

Paul says: Pauline will never agree to be his wife. Pauline hates George Mathis with a passion.

Pauline says: she will kill him before she will before she will marry Cole. Pauline despises him.

The elders tell Paul, Pasty, and Peggy: You must bring Pauline to me and let me talk to her. I have a plan that will stop George dead in his tracks.

Paul says: All right, I will do that after she gets home from work.

John says: All right. As a matter of fact, you all need to go ahead and eat dinner before you all come up.

Pasty, Peggy, and Paul all joined hands and orbed back to the manor. Peggy was so glad to see the manor was still standing. She walked into the kitchen and started cooking her meatloaf. Pasty walked into the kitchen and asked Peggy: You mind if I make the green salad?

Peggy says: Sure, if you want to, you can. Pasty says: Thanks! I love to make green salad.

Paul walked outside in the backyard and sat on a chair, enjoying some peace and quiet.

It was not long before Pauline and Pamela came walking in the door. Paul saw Pauline and Pamela and walked back into the manor and said, "Pauline, I need to talk to you and Pamela, please."

Pauline and Pamela walked outside with Paul and told them what had happened when Pasty and Peggy came home from work today. Pauline asks, "So when do we go see the elders?"

Paul says, "After dinner."

Pauline and Pamela said, "We need to change our clothes into something more comfortable."

Pauline and Pamela walked back into the manor and went upstairs to their bedrooms to change their clothes. Pauline walked into the bathroom, and when she came out, George was there in her room. Pauline looked at George and said, "Why are you here in my room? Whatever you want, the answer is no."

George says, "I want you to marry me."

Pauline looked him straight in the face and just busted out laughing. She laughed so hard that Pamela heard her, and it made Pamela go and check on Pauline. By the time Pamela walked in to

Pauline's room, Pamela saw George out of the corner of her eye, and she looked at him and said, "You are a dead man walking." George disappeared. Pamela walks over to Pauline and says, "Are you all right?"

Pauline says, "No! I am not all right." Pamela asks, "How can I help you?"

Pauline answers, "We need to go downstairs and tell the rest of the family what just happened."

Pamela says, "Okay, come on, I want to be there when we are explaining everything."

Pauline says, "You do realize when we tell Pasty, she is going to be so mad."

Pamela assured, "Yes, I know but one thing about it—she won't be mad at us."

Pauline says, "This is very true." Pamela says, "Pauline, take my hand." Pauline says, "All right."

Pamela and Pauline orbed downstairs into the kitchen, and Pauline went and got Paul and told him to come to the kitchen. Paul walked into the kitchen, and Pamela says, "You all are not going to believe what I am about to tell you, and I swear, every word is the truth."

Pasty says, "What is wrong?"

Pamela says, "When Pauline and I came home from work, we went upstairs to change our clothes after Paul told us what was going on. I went into my room, and Pauline went in to her room."

Pauline says, "I was getting ready to change into some shorts and a T-shirt when I looked up and saw George appear. He was sitting on my bed, and he told me that he would never stop until I agreed to marry him. I told him that will never happen. I also so told him that he was never going to hurt me or anyone else in my family. George looked me straight in the face and told me that he is in love with me. I looked him straight in the face and started laughing at him, and I told him I don't care how he feels nor do. I do not have any intentions of ever marrying him. I told him he is pure evil, and he will always be pure evil."

Pamela says, "I heard Pauline laughing so hard I decided to go and check what she was laughing at. As I walked into Pauline's room, I saw George Mathis out of the corner of my eye. That is when he disappeared."

Pasty says, "That evil little bastard. Who does he think he is, coming into our home without permission?"

Paul says, "Pasty, calm down, please. We must be able to think level headed not just anger."

Pasty says, "Paul, you are right, but that evil being just makes me so mad I want to hurt him badly."

Paul says, "Listen, someone is coming in the front door."

Pasty says, "I hope it is Mike."

Paul says, "Don't move. Let me see who it is." Paul walked in to the foyer and said to Mike, "I am glad that was you coming into the house."

Mike says, "Why? What is going on?"

Paul says, "Follow me and I will explain." Mike and Paul walked into the kitchen, and Paul explained everything to Mike.

Mike asks, "Okay, so what do we do next?"

Paul answers, "We all must go and see the elders after dinner. We want you to come with us, please."

Mike says, "Absolutely. I will go with you all. I want to go upstairs and change my clothes. Paul, you want to come with me, so we can talk?"

Paul says, "Just hurry up and come downstairs, and we can talk then."

Mike says, "Okay, I will be back soon." Mike went upstairs and changed his clothes.

Peggy finished cooking dinner, and Pauline and Pamela set the table for dinner. Paul walked into the kitchen. He walked over to his wife and took her by the hand, and he laid a lip-lock on her that made the rest of the sister's smile. Paul got down on one knee, and he proclaimed his love for his wife. Paul told Peggy she is a beautiful, sweet, and very kind-hearted and that is why he loves her as much as he does.

Peggy says: You are the best husband a girl could ask for. I am so very lucky to have you as my husband and my best friend. You are my soulmate always.

Paul says: Can I help you with anything, Peggy?

Peggy says, "Please get everyone to the dinner table so that we can sit down and enjoy our family and our dinner."

Paul says, "I can do that." Paul told everyone to come to the table, so they can eat.

Everyone went to the table and sat down to eat. While everyone was sitting at the table and they were fixing their plates of food, George was spying on the Williams family. George was invisible, so no one would be able to see him. George was making plans on when the best time to kidnap Peggy would be. George finally decided that after Pasty's wedding would be the best time. George wanted to do it once everyone was in bed sound asleep. That way, no one would know that Peggy was missing until they all woke up. George stood there and watched everyone eating, and he was listening to their conversation. Pauline turned around and look directly at where George was standing, and she said: George Mathis, I know you are watching all of us.

Pasty says: Where is he, Pauline?

Pauline says: He is standing right behind Mike.

Mike says: George Mathis, you are a low-down coward. You don't have the courage to come out of hiding to face us.

The moment Mike said that, George disappeared. Pauline says: I think you called his bluff, Mike.

Mike says: George is a coward. He is afraid of the Williams sisters. He is afraid of you, Pauline. Everyone continued to eat their dinner. Once dinner was done, Pasty and Pauline cleaned up the kitchen and the dining room. The rest of the gang walked into the living room, turned on the television, and started watching a good movie. As soon as Pasty and Pauline was done cleaning the kitchen and dining room, up they joined the rest of the family in the living room.

As they were sitting and watching their movie that they wanted to watch, they all heard a real loud noise as if a bomb had gone off. The noise came from outside. They all got up and ran out the back door to find out what the noise was. Mike looked at the roof of the manor, and he noticed that part of it was gone. Mike says: Pasty, look at the roof of the manor.

Pasty looked and said; What is going on with the manor?

Pauline says: I don't know, but this is very creepy.

Peggy says: I hope the manor is not falling apart.

Paul says: No, it is evil trying to scare us.

Pasty says: Well, if that is the case, whoever is responsible for this better be very afraid.

When Mike looked back at the roof of the manor, it was back. Everything was just as it was before the parts of the roof were missing. Mike says: This is so confusing. How are the evil allowed to do this to our home?

Pauline says: Apparently, evil can do anything they want.

Peggy says: Yes, and that is not fair nor that is right.

Paul says: I agree, but I did not make the rules that evil follows. Maybe I should orb up to the elders and see what they must say about all of this.

Pasty says: Can I go with you, Paul? Paul says: Of course, you can.

Pasty and Paul orbed up to the elders. They were gone for a while, and Peggy was in the kitchen getting dessert ready for everyone to have and enjoy. Paul and Pasty were gone for about an hour, and they orbed back to the manor and walked into the kitchen where Peggy was fixing some decaf coffee for her family. Pauline and Pamela were headed to the kitchen to see if they could help. Peggy told everyone to go to the table and get ready for dessert. Paul says: The elders had a lot to say about what is going on. Apparently, George is determined to have Pauline as his wife. The elders are sending someone named Carl Manning to help Pauline. Carl Manning is a cupid, and he is in love with Pauline. The elders want her to marry Carl Manning.

Pasty says: Carl Manning is cute, Pauline. He is very nice, and I have a good feeling you will love him dearly. Carl Manning will be the best thing that could happen to you. George won't know what to do if you marry Carl Manning.

Pamela says: That reminds me. I met a police officer today, and his name is Jack Marble. He is very good looking. He asks me out on a date for next Friday night.

Peggy says: Aw, that is so sweet. Are you going to go out with him?

Pamela says: Yes, I am going to go out with him. We are going to the movies.

Pasty says: I hope it is a good movie. Pamela says: Yes, it is a comedy.

Pasty says: Oh, I bet it will be good.

It was getting late, and everyone was getting tired. They all needed to find their beds and get in them. The Williams sisters were always so busy killing demons and other evil demotic until when ten pm rolled around all the girls were ready to lie down and get some sleep. Everyone started upstairs and went to bed. It was not long before Paul, Mike, and Pauline came back to the manor. Paul, Mike, and Pauline went straight upstairs to bed.

As everyone was sleeping, the Williams sisters had peaceful sleep. Paul and Mike were resting good when they both heard a noise, and they both got up to investigate. Paul and Mike search the whole house, including the attic. There was nothing wrong.

Paul says, "We must go outside and make sure everything is all right."

Mike says, "I will get two flashlights so that we will be able to see."

Paul says, "That is a good idea."

Mike walked in to the laundry room and brought two flashlights out for Paul and him. Paul and Mike walked out the back door and shined the flashlights on top of the manor, so they could be sure that the roof was overall house. Everything seemed to be where it was supposed to be, and then Paul says, "We might as well go back into the manor and make sure it is all locked up, and then we can go back to bed and rest."

Mike says, "Good idea."

That is exactly what Paul and Mike did. They went back into the manor and made sure all the doors and windows were locked up tight. Then they both went back upstairs to their rooms and went to bed.

It did not take Mike and Paul to fall back to sleep, and they rested good. Peggy had her alarm set so that she would be able to get up and have coffee and breakfast made for her whole family. It was seven thirty in the morning. It was a beautiful Saturday morning. Peggy got up and quietly walked into their bathroom, and she shut the door so that Paul would not hear the shower going and he could rest more. Peggy was being very quiet, and just as she was coming out of the bathroom, she stepped on a squeaky toy of Jonathan's. She jumped because it scared her. She was so surprised that it did not wake Paul up. All Paul did was turn over on his stomach. Paul did not even open his eyes. He just rolled over and was sleeping nicely. Peggy managed to pick up the toy, and she was dressed for being at home, so she closed the bedroom door and quietly walked downstairs so that she could go ahead and start the coffee. She made pancakes for breakfast along with fruit cups and orange juice and bacon. Soon, everyone was downstairs. The dining room table was set, and everyone was sitting down enjoying their breakfast. Peggy says: I was thinking that we all could go to Golden Gate park and spend the day just enjoying nature.

Mike says: We should go camping in the mountains.

Pasty says: That sounds like a lot of fun, but I would love to go to the park so that we would at least be around in case of a demon attack or something.

Pamela says: Why not stay home, and we can be there in case of a demon, but we can pretend we are in a cabin camping. As a matter of fact, we can turn the manor into a cottage if you want, or we could just pretend the manor is a cabin.

Peggy says: That sounds good to me. We can even not answer the phone nor the door either.

Pasty says: I like you guys idea.

Paul says: So, we are all in agreement for our weekend?

Everyone says: Yes, we all want to do this plan.

Even though everyone agreed with the plans for the weekend, Pasty, Peggy, Pauline, Pamela, Paul, and Mike knew deep down in their hearts that evil could strike at any time. They all knew that they were always in the sight of the demons. Evil seemed to find them know matter where they are. That is why when Pamela came up with the idea of camping out at the manor. Everyone loved the idea. Pasty, Peggy, Pauline, and Pamela decided that they would decorate the manor as if it were a cabin they were renting. Paul and Mike went out into the backyard and cleaned up the grill. They also cleaned up the backyard and made it look like a cabin they were renting.

Once Pasty, Peggy, Pauline, and Pamela were done with decorating the manor to look like a cabin, Peggy went into the kitchen and started making a list of things she needed at the store. Once Peggy wrote out her grocery order, she walked out to the backyard and told Paul: I am going grocery shopping. I will be back soon.

Paul says: All right, we will be right here when you get back.

Peggy asked Pasty to go with her shopping, and Pasty says: Of course, I will go with you. Let me tell Mike so he won't wonder where I am.

Pasty walked outside and told Mike what she was going to do. Mike says: Okay, have fun you two.

Pasty turned toward Mike and smiled at him. Mike smiled back at Pasty and winked his left eye. Pasty then turned and walked out the front door of the manor. She walked over to Peggy's car and opened the car door. She got into the car and shut the door, and off they both went to the grocery store. While Pasty and Peggy were at the store grocery shopping Pamela, Paul, and Pauline were setting up crystals to protect the manor from vanishing and to keep evil away for the two days they were pretending to be in a cabin. Once Pamela, Paul, and Pauline set the crystals out except for one until Pasty and Peggy came back from the store. Pauline walked into the kitchen and was making a green salad to go with what they were going to have with supper, which was grilled cheeseburgers and French fries. Once Pauline was done making the salad, she proceeded to peel some potatoes for the French fries. Once Pauline was done with that, she put the sliced-up potatoes in a big bowl with cold water. Then she walked into the living room and sat down and started watching some television. Pamela walked into the kitchen and took everything she would need to set the table, so they would be able to enjoy their meal.

Pasty and Peggy were unloading the groceries from their cart into the trunk of Peggy's car when out of nowhere, George appeared. Pasty walked in front of Peggy so that Pasty could help Peggy just in case George tried to hurt Peggy. George looked straight at Pasty and Peggy. George says: You can't keep me from Pauline. She will be my wife one way or another.

Pasty says, "Really, George, is that all you intend to do, whine? Because you don't seem to get it that Pauline doesn't want you. Pauline does not want you because you are completely pure evil inside and out."

Peggy says, "George, you know that we will stop you from marrying our sister. Pauline says she wants nothing to do with you or your evil ways."

Pasty says, "But since I know you won't believe us, come by the manor, and Pauline will straighten you out on a few facts."

George says, "Every one of you thinks you are so much better than me. Just because I am evil, you don't like me."

Peggy says, "George, you got that right. None of us like you at all. We don't want you around either."

Chapter 8

Oh No, Not Again

THE WILLIAMS SISTERS HAD BEEN WORKING FOR ABOUT two months, and they needed to take some time off so that they could get everything set up for Pasty and Mike's wedding. Pasty, Peggy, Pauline, and Pamela already had daytime managers to run their businesses, so they could at least take two weeks off from work. Now Pasty and Peggy had already lined up the florists and the caterer for the wedding. Pauline had already asked Grand to ask their mother to attend Pasty and Mike's wedding. Grand had already asked the angel of destiny to perform the wedding ceremony, and she had agreed to do the ceremony for Pasty and Mike. Mike already asked Paul to be his best man. Paul said he would be honored to stand with Mike on this very important day.

It was a Saturday night, and Carl Manning asked Pauline out. She was looking forward to spending some time with Carl Manning.

Now the Williams sisters and their family had not heard from George in a while. They all knew that George would never leave Pauline alone if Pauline was not married to Carl Manning. Pauline was dressed and ready to go out with Carl Manning. Carl Manning appeared in the Williams manor, and he was being chased by a demon who had already tried his best to kill Carl Manning if Pauline and Carl Manning were not married. While everyone was home at the manor and Pauline was standing right next to Carl Manning. Carl Manning took out his ring that he bought for Pauline He knelt on one knee and took Pauline's hand. Carl Manning says: You are the only one for me. Pauline Williams, will you marry me?

Pauline says: Yes, yes, yes, I will marry you!

Pamela had been dating a man named Jack Marble for a while. Carl Manning had already asked Paul to be his best man. Mike had already asked Daryl to be his best man. Pasty had already asked Peggy to be her maid of honor. Pauline had already asked Pamela to be her maid of honor.

Now the Williams sisters had not seen George for a while. They kind of thought that George might try to interfere with the double wedding that was going to be taking place real soon. The double weddings were one month away. The Williams sisters were trying to keep their house as clean as possible. The sisters were pretending to be staying in a cabin for the weekend so that maybe they could just have some family time together.

Mike was very happy that there was going to be another wedding in the family. Mike always thought that the Williams sisters should all be married and be happy in their life.

Now the charmed ones had been working hard on keeping the manor picked up. They were trying to keep everything as cleaned up as possible, so they would not have to spend all day cleaning and setting up for their double wedding.

Pasty had bought her a wedding dress, and Pauline was planning on wearing their mother's wedding dress. Pauline had already sent the wedding dress to be dry cleaner so that it would be ready and beautiful for their wedding day.

Paul, Carl Manning, and Mike had already gone and picked out their tuxes for the wedding. They already tried them on, and they fit just right.

Peggy, Pasty, and Pauline had already gone to the wedding cake store and placed their orders. Their cakes would be there on June 1 for their wedding.

Pasty and Peggy made it home from the grocery store. Paul and Mike brought in the groceries, and Pauline and Pamela put the groceries away. Peggy made hamburgers and took out the hot dogs. Once Peggy was done making the hamburgers, she made some mac and cheese along with green salad and garlic toast. Pauline made fresh tea. Pamela set the dining room table so that they could all sit down and enjoy their meal and their family time.

While Pasty and Peggy were at the grocery store, Pauline and Pamela made a chocolate cake with chocolate frosting on it. They had just finished with the cake when Pasty and Peggy came home from the store.

Suddenly, there was a knock at the door. Mike walked over to the door and answered it. It was Cole. George was looking for Pauline. Mike told George he was not welcome here at the manor. George looked at Mike as if he wanted to destroy him. Mike told him if he did not leave, he would regret it. Suddenly, Pasty and Peggy, along with Pauline and Pamela, walked to the front door, and they all told George he was not welcome in their home because he is pure evil. George was so mad, so he disappeared. Mike shut the door. Paul and Mike went outside to cook the hamburgers and hot dogs for their family. Peggy walked back into the kitchen so that she could make sure she had everything ready for the food to be put on the table once the meat was done. It took about twenty minutes, and the meat was all done. Everyone came to the table. They all sat down at the dinner table and fixed their plates.

Peggy says: Well, I am so glad that you all are enjoying this meal. Just wait for dessert.

Pauline says: Don't tell the guys that. Peggy says: Why not?

Pauline says: You will spoil the surprise.

Peggy says: What, you don't think the guys know that we have a nice dessert?

Pauline says: Yes, I am sure they do. Peggy says: Don't be so silly, Pauline.

So as each one of them would finish their meal, they would get up from the table and pick up their plate and silverware and their glass that they were drinking out of and take it into the kitchen on the counter by the sink. Then they would walk out of the kitchen and go into the living room and watch some television. Soon, everyone was in the living room except for Pauline and Pamela. They were cleaning up the dining room and the kitchen. Paul walked into the kitchen and was checking to see if the garbage needs to be taken out. Pauline was rinsing out the dishes in the kitchen, loading up the dishwasher, and Pamela was bringing all the food and other things that was on the dining room table so that she could wipe the table off and go into the kitchen and put the leftover food away. It took Pauline a good forty-five minutes to get the dining room and kitchen all cleaned up, and then Pauline and Pamela went into the living room where everyone else was at, and they watched television.

Pamela received a phone call from the guy she was dating, Jack Marble. Jack Marble wanted to take Pamela out to the movies. Pamela got ready, and Jack Marble came and picked her up from the manor, and they went to a movie.

George Mathis appeared at the front door of the manor. George knocked on the door, and Paul got up and walked to the front door. Paul placed his hand on the door knob, and when Paul opened the door, he found George standing there. Peggy started walking to the front door to see who it was, and as soon as she saw George, Peggy turned around and to her sisters Pasty, Pamela, and Pauline to hurry because George is at the door. As all four Williams sisters walked up to the door, George looked at them and said: I will marry Pauline she will be my wife.

Pauline says: Not going to happen, George Mathis. I will never marry someone as evil as you are.

George looks at Pauline with such evil in his heart, and Pauline feels the evil radiating off Cole. Pauline looks at George and says: I will never be your queen of evil. Never going to happen.

With that, George vanishes, and the Williams sisters turn and walk back to the living room. Paul soon follows. Peggy walks into the kitchen and slices everyone a piece of cake and puts it on a saucer along with a fork and a coffee cup for everyone. It was time for dessert, and Pasty walked into the kitchen and started setting the table for everyone to enjoy the cake and decaf coffee. Once the coffee was done, Peggy walked into the living room and told everyone to come get their dessert.

As everyone was sitting at the dining room and eating their cake, George appeared and says: I don't believe you will keep me from having a talk with Pauline.

Pauline says: Sure, George, we can have a conversation, but I am not moving from this spot I am in. Besides that, I want my sisters to hear what you must say. By the way, George, this is Carl Manning, my boyfriend, who I am getting married to June 1 of this year.

George says: How can you do that to me, Pauline? I don't understand why you won't even go out with me.

Pauline says: Because you are evil and just plain mean. You never wanted to be a good person. You have been evil since you were a young man.

George says: Yes, this is very true but, the source of all evil is the one who turned me evil.

Pasty says: Yes, but you had a choice in the matter. You could have walked away from the source of all evil.

George says: You are wrong about that. The source of all evil has been holding my father's spirit to lure me over to his side to do his evil bidding.

Pauline says: It does not matter because I don't love you. I am in love with Carl Manning, and there is nothing you can do to make me marry you. Even if you do something mean to hurt Carl Manning or kill him, I will still never marry you, Cole.

George looked at all the Williams sisters sitting at the table, and even he had his doubts about being able to beat the Williams sisters. George looked at Pauline and said: Until you are married, I will do everything in my power to make sure you and Carl Manning are never married.

George vanished, and everyone continued eating their dessert. Once dessert was done, Pamela cleaned up the dining room and the kitchen. Pauline went upstairs and took a shower. Carl Manning came upstairs soon after and told Pauline he would be back tomorrow. Carl Manning gave Pauline a hug and a kiss, and then he left.

George is so mad he could eat nail, and all that anger held in side for George is a good thing. The Williams sisters know that he can and will kill if he decides to. Not only can George shimmer, but he can also go underground where the other demons are and enlist them to help him. George can assign demons to cause death to the Williams sisters and their other family members.

Pauline was in love with Carl Manning. She did not want to go with anybody else. She was planning on being Carl Manning's wife. Pauline was not studying anyone else. Paul and Mike were getting tired of the way George was threating Pauline and the other sisters as well. Even Jack Marble thought that George was acting like a butthead. Jack Marble did not like the way he was treating any of the other sisters.

Pamela and Jack Marble made it back from the movies. Jack Marble dropped Pamela off at the manor. Pamela walked in to the living room and says: Good night.

Pamela then turns around and walks up stairs to her room and goes to bed. It was not long before all the Williams sisters and their boyfriends were in bed fast asleep.

As everyone was slowly drifting off to sleep, the manor fell in to a very peaceful mood, as if peace was drifting everyone off to sleep. There was absolutely no noise in or about the manor. The only sound that could be heard was sleep. Before everyone had drifted off to their pleasant sleep, they all had set their alarms, so they would be able to be up and ready for church. Tomorrow was indeed a Sunday, and they were going to church.

As everyone was sleeping so peacefully, they all had good dreams, not with a lot of evil involved but more like a wishful dream of marriage, family, and life in general.

Pauline, however, had a dream pertaining to her and Pasty having a double wedding. Pasty and Mike also had a dream about Pauline and Carl Manning being married but on a different wedding day. As the night ended and daybreak was starting, Pauline woke up from her dream, and she called Carl Manning's name. Carl Manning appeared in Pauline's bedroom. Pauline told Carl Manning that she wanted to get married to him, but not on Pasty and Mike's wedding day. Pauline says: Pasty and Mike's wedding day needs to be very special, and you and I can get married the following month on July 16.

Carl Manning says, "Pauline, you are correct about Pasty and Mike's wedding being special. That is part of the reason why the elders let Pasty and Mike come back."

Pauline says, "Yes, I know. That is why I need your help in convincing Pasty and Mike to let us have our wedding separate from their wedding. I want you to come over after church. Can you come around two this afternoon?"

Carl Manning says, "I sure can, and I will be here." Carl Manning leans into Pauline and gives her a great big kiss, and then he vanished.

Peggy's alarm went off, so she turned off her alarm and quietly got out of bed and headed toward the bathroom. The night before, Peggy had already picked out the outfit she will be wearing to church and placed it in the bathroom so that she would be able to get her shower and head downstairs to make coffee, family to get a shower and get dressed and she headed to the kitchen so that she would be ready to feed her family.

Just as Pauline and Pasty started walking out of their bedrooms, they turned toward each other, and Pauline walked over to Pasty and says, "Pasty, I don't want you to take this the wrong way, but I think, as a matter of fact, you should have your wedding separate from mine. In other words, I want you to go ahead and have your wedding as planned, and Carl Manning and I want to wait a while before we get married."

Pasty says, "Are you sure, Pauline?" Pauline says, "Yes, we are all sure."

Pasty says, "All right, I will tell Mike and Peggy, along with the rest of the gang, this morning while we are eating breakfast."

Pauline says, "That sounds good to me."

Both Pauline and Pasty walked down the stairs toward the kitchen. As Pasty and Pauline walked into the kitchen and started taking all the food and plates and silverware to set the breakfast up for the family, Pasty says, "I have an announcement to make. Pauline and I have been talking, and we have decided that we will have separate weddings. Mine is still set for June 1, and Pauline wants to wait a year and a half before they get married."

Pauline says, "This is what Carl Manning and I really want."

Pasty says, "If everyone agrees, we shall do exactly what Pauline and Carl Manning want to do."

Peggy says, "I am planning on fixing meatloaf, mashed Potatoes, gravy, garlic toast, green salad, and tea to drink with our dinner. How does that sound to everyone?"

Pasty, Mike, Peggy, Paul, Pauline, Carl Manning, and Pamela all said, "Sounds good to all of us."

Pasty says, "All right, everyone who is going to church load up and let's go."

Everyone left, except for Paul. It is not that Paul did not want to go to church, but he knew he was always on call from the elders, and they would orb him up anytime.

Pasty and Mike got into Pasty's car, and off to church they went. Peggy and Pamela rode together. Pauline and Carl Manning got into Pauline's car, and off to church they went.

Paul went upstairs and started cleaning. All the bedrooms were cleaned up and the beds were all made up by Paul. He then proceeded downstairs and started cleaning up the kitchen. The living room was not dirty, so the rest of the house was clean, and all Paul needed to do was to take out all the trash, which he did.

Paul had everything done, and he went into the kitchen to make sure everything was cleaned up. He then walked over to the refrigerator and opened it and took out the tea pitcher and got himself a glass out. He poured himself a glass of tea and made himself a sandwich. Paul took the tea and the sandwich into the living room and turned on the television and started watching some news.

It was about thirty minutes later when Pasty, Mike, Peggy, Pamela, Pauline, and Carl Manning came home to the manor. Pasty and Mike pulled into their parking spot so that Mike would be able to get out to go to work tomorrow morning at 6:00 a.m. Pamela and Peggy pulled into Peggy's parking spot. Pauline and Carl Manning pulled into their parking spot. They all got out of their cars and started walking to the front door, and Peggy open it. As she started walking inside the house, she noticed how nice and clean the manor was. The manor was fixed up nice and normal. In other words, the manor was the manor, not a cabin for the weekend.

Chapter 9

Demons and More Demons

THE DAWN WAS BREAKING, AND EVERYONE WAS IN peaceful sleep. Peggy, Pasty, Pauline, and Pamela all had their alarms set to wake them up at 7:00 a.m. so that they would all have plenty of time to shower and get dressed for work. Peggy is usually the first one up and taking her shower first. Once she is done with getting her shower and getting dressed for her day it was Monday, so Peggy knew she would be going to work. Soon as Peggy was dressed, and her makeup was own, she headed downstairs to make the coffee. Meanwhile, Pasty was just getting out of the shower and getting dressed for work.

Pauline was up and getting into the shower. Pauline will also be getting dressed for work. Pasty was already downstairs and had her cup of coffee and muffin for breakfast while reading the newspaper. Pauline soon was downstairs with her coffee and her bowl for cereal for her breakfast. Pamela was just getting into her shower, and Paul was up and getting ready to take a shower too. Once Paul was done with his shower and he left the bedroom Paul made sure that the bathroom was cleaned up, and the bed was made. Then Paul walked downstairs and to the kitchen so that he could have him some coffee and breakfast. Paul cleaned up the kitchen and orbed off to the magic school.

While everyone was at work, Pauline was sitting at her desk, and she was working on a plan to nail George Mathis and finally get rid of him for good. That was part of the reason Pauline and Carl Manning decided that it was time to stop George from ever trying to hurt Pauline again.

Pauline knew how George thought she knew that she, along with her sister, could permanently put a stop to him. Pauline also knew that once she figured out the plan, all she would have to do is to let her sisters in on it, and they would love the opportunity to destroy George and stop some of the madness that was going on with all the demons.

As a matter of fact, all the sisters, while they were at work, had George on their mind. Pasty really wanted to go after George. She did not trust him, nor did she like him. Pasty always had a very bad feeling about George. She knew he was pure evil all the way through. Pasty remembered from before she died how she did not like Cole. Pasty remembered how George hurt Pauline in so many ways. Pasty just wanted the evil man gone away forever. Pasty, Peggy, Pauline, nor Pamela never liked him. No one seemed to like Cole.

While everyone was at work, George magically appeared in the attic. George was still trying to figure out how to make Peggy more comfortable while she was in the underworld after Pasty and Mike's wedding. Suddenly, George spotted the dollhouse that was the Williams manor that was sitting on the table in the attic. That was when George finally realized what he would have to do to make Peggy be calmer while he held her underground so that George would be able to stop any chance of Pauline marrying anyone but him. George wanted to be her husband, and he wanted Pauline to be his queen of the night. None of the girls were aware that George had this kind of intentions toward the Williams sisters. Pasty hated him, every inch of him. Pasty knew how mean and evil George Mathis was. Once George had his idea, he vanished into thin air. Once again, the Williams manor was free of pure evil. It was around noontime, and the Williams sisters had an hour off for lunch. So, Pamela orbed to where Pasty worked and then on to Peggy's and Pauline's work. Then they all orbed to the manor where they find Paul home, and he had made lunch for everyone, which was all the leftovers in the fridge. Pasty walked over to the counter where Paul had set up all the plates and silverware and glasses so that everyone could fix their plate and grab their glass of tea and go to the dining room table and sit down and eat their lunch. Pasty, Pauline, and Pamela sat on one side of the dinner table, and Peggy and Paul sat on the other side of the dinner table so that they could all eat their lunch and hurry off back to work. Once everyone was done eating, Pasty, Pauline, Peggy, and Pamela all held hands, and off to work they all orbed. Paul had just enough time to load the dishwasher and get it started, and he had managed to clean up the kitchen and dining room. Once Paul was done with that, he then orbed off to the magic school so that he could finish his day of teaching the young witches.

The afternoon seemed to fly by. Every one of the Williams sisters worked all afternoon, and they were all ready to come home to the manor, so they could have some good family time. Paul was through with all his classes that he needed to teach, so he orbed to the manor. The moment Paul orbed into the kitchen, he was happy because now he would be able to get the grill ready. He fixed himself a nice glass of iced tea. Once, Paul got his glass of tea, he walked out the back door and started setting up the grill. The steaks had already been taken out and all thawed out. Paul went ahead and marinated the steaks, so they would be ready to place on the grill. It wasn't long after that when Pasty and Peggy came pulling up in the driveway. Pasty and Peggy picked up their purses and keys and opened their car doors so that they could get out and go into the manor. Pasty and Peggy was very glad to be home. They had a very busy day. Pasty and Peggy walked into the kitchen and found that Paul had already washed the steaks and had them marinating. Peggy walked over to where she kept eight nice-sized potatoes and took them over to the sink to wash them. Pasty walked over to the refrigerator opened it, and she took out the lettuce, tomatoes, purple onion, olives, and cucumber so that she could make a nice green salad. Peggy started a pot of fresh tea also. Mike walked out back with Paul, and they were talking about the grill. Mike told Paul: You are getting good at using the grill.

Paul says: Why, thank you. I really love cooking on the grill.

Paul says: Mike, would you go into the kitchen and get the potatoes that Peggy has wrapped in foil and bring them out here to me so that we can start cooking them?

Mike says: Sure, I will do that.

Meanwhile, Pauline and Pamela came home from work, and they walked straight upstairs and changed their clothes. As Pauline and Pamela were on their way downstairs Pauline says: We should walk into the kitchen and see what is going on. Maybe we can go ahead and set the table for dinner.

Pamela says: That is a very good idea. Our guys will be coming home soon.

Pauline says; I sure hope George stays away from me.

Pamela says: That would be very nice, but I would not hold my breath on that idea.

Pauline says: You are correct. There' no telling what George will do. I have a plan that I want to talk over with everybody at dinner.

Pauline and Pamela walked into the kitchen, and they saw that Peggy and Pasty was fixing dinner, so Pauline and Pamela went ahead and got everything they would need to set the table.

Peggy says: Hi, Pamela, how was your day at the club?

Pamela says: It was actually very nice, and I really love the night manager that you hired. As a matter of fact, the whole staff is good.

Peggy says: Well, I am glad that everything is working out. So how are you liking running the club.

Pamela says: It is good. I am learning and loving every moment of it.

It was not long before Jack Marble came driving up to the manor. Carl Manning orbed into the living room just as Jack Marble came walking into the front door of the manor. Paul and Mike came walking into the manor and told Peggy that they were about ready to put all the steak on the grill. Peggy had already taken the steak out of the marinade and put them on a cookie sheet pan so that Paul would be able to carry the pans, and Mike would carry the other pan out to the grill. While Paul and Mike were doing that, Pauline walked out back; and when one of the cookie sheet pans were empty back into the manor so that Peggy would wash it and get a plate so that Paul would be able to fit all the steaks on the platter and it could go on the dinner table. Peggy had Pauline bring a nice size bowl out to the grill, so the potatoes could be put in the bowl. Pauline did exactly what Peggy ask her to do. She walked back into the manor and toward the kitchen where Pasty and Peggy were. Peggy was taking the green salad that Pasty had made and handed it to Pauline to put on the dining room table. Pamela walked into the kitchen and grabbed an ice bucket and filled it up with ice. Pamela then walked into the dining room and started filling up all the glasses around the table so that everyone would be able to enjoy a glass of tea with their dinner.

After Pamela was all done putting ice in the glasses, it was not long before Pauline and Pasty were bringing the baked potatoes along with the steaks that Paul had cooked on the grill into the manor and on the dining room table so that everyone would be able to sit down and have a nice super with the family. Peggy had made some yeast rolls for dinner. Once dinner was cooked and the table was ready, and Peggy told everyone to come so they could eat. As Pasty, Mike, Peggy, Paul, Pauline, Carl Manning, Pamela, and Jack Marble were all sitting at the table, Pasty started fixing her plate, and she was passing the food around the table. Suddenly they all hear a woman's voice screaming. They all jumped up from the table, and Mike said: Good Lord, what is wrong?

Mike took off running out the front door of the manor. Paul Orbed to the attic. Pasty, Peggy, Pauline, and Pamela ran out to the backyard, and it did not matter where everyone was. They could hear the woman screaming bloody murder. Mike ran and grabbed his cell phone and called the police department. Paul orbed up to the elders to see if they knew what was going on. The elders had no clue. S, Paul orbed back the manor and walked out back to find the sisters looking around to see what was going on. They all ran out to the road and started looking around. Pauline raised up her arms, and she started to rise and fly. Pauline was not concerned that someone would see her. She was concerned about the woman screaming bloody murder. Pauline got a prementioned the voice of the screaming was from evil who was threaten a young witch. Pasty, Peggy, Pauline, and Pamela all ran to the attic. Pauline told her sister she had a prementioned.

Peggy says: What was it?

Pauline says: This woman voices we are. Do you know who this person is? I have seen her around, but I just can' place where.

Pasty says, "Pauline, please try to remember where you saw this lady at."

Pauline says, "I seem to remember. She was at a job site you were working on taking some pictures of a statue."

Pasty says, "Oh, oh yes, I remember."

Pauline says, "Pasty, try to remember her name."

Pasty is thinking hard, and as she is thinking, she walks toward the kitchen. Pasty then turns around and says, "I remember her name. It was Stella."

Pauline runs up the stairs to the attic where she finds the book of shadows. Pasty, Peggy, and Pamela ran up the stairs to the attic also. As Pasty, Peggy, and Pamela walked into the attic, Pauline says: I wanted to check in the book of shadows to see if there was a spell involving the name Stella.

Peggy says: Well, is there? Pauline says: Sadly, no.

Pasty says: Pauline, why were you asking about Stella anyway? I just realized something about the spirit that has been chasing after Peggy.

Pauline says: That Stella seemed to be attracted to Peggy, and I don't mean sexual either. I mean intellectually.

Peggy says: Wait, what are you saying?

Pauline says: Relax, Peggy, she liked to have good conversation with you.

Peggy says: Oh. Okay, I understand, I think.

Pasty says: Don't worry, Peggy. I will explain it later.

Finally, the screaming from the woman stopped, and the Williams sisters and husbands, along with boyfriends, all turn around and came downstairs.

Everyone was very hungry, and they were all ready to eat. Pasty and Mike came downstairs first. As they walked over to the dining room table, Mike pulled out Pasty's chair for her. Just as she was getting ready to sit down, Peggy and Paul walked over to the table, and they also sat down. Pauline and Carl Manning, along with

Pamela and Jack Marble, came downstairs and joined everyone at the dining room table. Pasty started fixing her plate and passed the food around the table to make sure everyone would have plenty of food to eat. Pasty, Peggy, Pauline, Pamela, Paul, Mike, Carl Manning, and Jack Marble always enjoyed their food and company at the dining room table at the Williams sisters' home. Once each one of them that would finish their plates and clear their dishes from the table, and they would walk their dishes into the kitchen. Once dinner was done, everyone, except for Pamela and Pauline, went into the living room to watch television. Pamela walked into the kitchen and started her dishwasher. Pauline cleaned off the dining room table and brought all the leftover food into the kitchen. Pauline sat it all on the counter so that she could put away the leftover food in the right-size bowl with the proper lid to be put in the refrigerator. Once Pauline had cleared the dining room table, she wiped it down and started putting up the leftover food in the refrigerator. Pamela washed off all the dishes and loaded up the dishwasher, so the dish would be sanitized. That is how the Williams sisters keep all sickness away, so they can do their regular jobs and their magical jobs as good witches.

Once Pamela and Pauline were all done with cleaning up the kitchen and the dining room, they too went into the living room and started watching television with the rest of the family. They were all watching a comedy on television, and they all enjoyed it completely. Once the movie was over with, they all decided it was time for bed. All four of the Williams sisters walked upstairs to their bedrooms. The four guys walk through the manor and checked all the windows to make sure they were locked. Before Paul locked the back door, he took the garbage out and then walked back into the manor and locked the back door. Mike locked the front door. Once they were done with that, they all went upstairs to the attic to make sure everything was all right. Paul set the alarm around the book of shadows just in case some evil demon wanted to steal it.

Now that Paul, Mike, Carl Manning, and Jack Marble knew the manor was safe, they all decided it was time for bed. Jack Marble went to Pamela's room, got in his jammies, crawled in bed, and went to sleep. Jack Marble had his alarm set for 5:00 a.m. because he needed to be up and ready for work by 6:00 a.m. so that he would be on shift through the police department by 7:00 a.m.

Carl Manning had walked into Pauline's room, and his alarm was set for 7:30 a.m. so that he could be on Love's duty by 8:00 a.m. Mike went to Pasty's room. His alarm was set for 5: 00 a.m. so that he could be to work by 7:00 a.m. Paul went into Peggy's room, put his jammies on, and crawled in bed with Peggy, who was fast asleep. Paul's alarm was set for 7: 30 a.m. so that he'll be ready for work by 8: 00 a.m. so that Paul could be at magic school to teach his classes.

Pasty, Peggy, Pauline, and Pamela were all fast asleep, and their alarms was set for 7:00 a.m. so that they would be able to have breakfast and discuss whatever they needed to for the day.

Now everyone is in bed sleeping peacefully and having pleasant dreams. While they are all sleeping, evil is prowling through the manor. The evil is Cole, but this time, George is outside the manor also looking at how it is put together. George wanted to make sure that once he had set up the evil Williams manor, it would look just like the regular Williams manor. While George was inside the manor, no one could see him. George was writing down everything that was inside the Williams manor. He made sure he had all the details concerning the items that were in it, just like the construction of the Williams manor. George wanted it to be able to fool the Williams sisters completely. George had finally decided on how he would proceed with his plans. George had every intention of kidnapping each one of the Williams sisters and holding them hostage. George thought he could pull of the biggest demon attack against the good witches, the Williams sisters.

As the night ended and the dawn was breaking, there was a slight breeze blowing a slight sweet smell in the air. It was just about 7:00 a.m., and Pasty, Peggy, Pauline, and Pamela's alarm went off. Pasty laid in bed for about fifteen minutes, while Peggy was up and taking her shower, which only took about eight minutes. That way, Pasty was assured to have hot water for her shower. While Peggy was getting dressed and ready for work, Pasty was taking her shower. Pauline laid in bed until seven thirty. That way, she would be able to take her shower. Pamela waited until Pauline was done before she took her shower.

Meanwhile, Peggy was downstairs making coffee for her family. Peggy had already taken out bowl for cereal for anyone who wanted some. It was not long before all the Williams sisters was downstairs having coffee and cereal before heading out to work. Paul was upstairs getting his shower, and just about the time the Williams sisters were ready to leave for work, Paul came downstairs to kiss his wife goodbye for the day.

As all the Williams sisters got into their cars and left for work Paul made him a bowl of cereal and a nice cup of coffee. Once Paul was done eating his breakfast, he cleaned up the kitchen, making sure he turns the coffee maker off. Paul took out the garbage. Once he was back in the manor, he orbed upstairs to put his shoes on so that he would be ready for work. Once Paul was ready for work, he orbed to the magical school where he taught young witches how to use their powers, so they would grow up and become good witches as adults.

While everyone was at work, George Mathis returned to the manor to continue making his notes. Now George knew that the Williams manor was on the Nexis of good.

Chapter 10

Here We Go Again

PEGGY WAKES UP AND GOES INTO THE BATHROOM to take a shower and get dressed. She heads downstairs to the kitchen to start preparing breakfast for her family. The rest of the Williams sisters are upstairs getting up and ready for their day. They all worked Monday through Friday. They always had the weekends off, except for Paul. Sometimes the elders would need him to help another witch that is coming into his or her powers.

It was not long before Peggy had the coffee fixed and the cereal bowls out along with spoons to eat their cereal if they wanted. Pasty, Pauline, and Pamela came walking downstairs headed to the kitchen for coffee. Paul was just getting out of the shower, and Peggy was ready to leave for work. They all had their coffee, and Pauline had a bowl of fruit loops cereal for breakfast. Just about the time Paul came walking downstairs, they were all getting up from the table so that they could leave for work. When Paul walked into the kitchen, he had just enough time to give his wife a kiss, and out the door the Williams sisters walked to get in their cars to go to work.

Paul watched his wife leave for work, and then he poured himself a cup of coffee and ate him a bowl of cereal. Once Paul was done eating, he cleaned up the kitchen and made sure the coffee pot was off and the trash was out. Paul went back upstairs to the attic to make sure everything was all right and the alarm was set around the book of shadows. Once Paul was done with that, he then orbed downstairs to make sure all the windows and doors was locked. Once that was done Paul walked into the kitchen to make sure that the chicken had been taken out for dinner. Once Paul was done, he orbed off to magic school for work.

Peggy had a lady come in to her restaurant who was wanting to a television on Peggy's restaurant and Peggy's night club. This lady that came in was a rich young snob who instantly did not like Peggy. This lady was someone who went to school with Peggy and did not like Pasty at all. This lady only tried to make a name for herself. Peggy called Pasty to tell her what was going on and who the lady was. Pasty recalled the lady and told Peggy she should not get involved with the lady because she always felt like that lady thought she was better than anyone else. Peggy agreed not to blow the lady off and tell her that she was way too busy to even consider doing a television show about cooking. The lady turned around and stuck her nose in the air and stomped off toward the front door when the she tripped over her two feet and fell flat on her face. The cashier walked over to the lady and helped her out, and Peggy was worried that evil was behind what had happened.

Peggy had already taken out the chicken for dinner tonight. She was going to have fried chicken, mashed potatoes, fresh green beans, fresh green salad, fresh yeast rolls, and fresh tea to go with their dinner. Peggy was planning on baking some brownies for dessert.

Peggy gets back to work, and so does Pasty. They worked the rest of their day. While they were all at work, George was messing around in the attic. He was all most caught by the crystals that

Paul had set around the book of shadows to keep evil from trying to steal it.

It was about four thirty in the afternoon. It was time for Paul to orb back home to the Williams manor. When Paul orbed to the manor, he landed right at the top of the stairs, so he went right into his room and changed into some shorts and a T-shirt. Paul went downstairs and headed out the back door so that Paul could get the trash cans and put them where they're supposed to go. Paul then went downstairs to the kitchen and peeled the potatoes for Peggy. After Paul was done peeling the potatoes, he washed them and put them in a pot with plenty of water.

Paul walked into the living room and started watching television until Peggy and Pasty came home. Peggy and Pasty went upstairs and changed their clothes. Pasty brought in the mail. She had received a letter from her cousin Jack. After Peggy was done changing her clothes, she proceeded downstairs so that she could prepare an awesome dinner for her family. Pasty stayed upstairs to read her letter Jack wrote her. Jack told Pasty they would be there the day after her wedding. Jack also told Pasty: Thank you for finding a home for my family.

Once Pasty finished reading her letter, she walked back downstairs and headed to the kitchen to see if Peggy needed any helping with dinner. Pasty says: Peggy, can I help you fix dinner?

Peggy says, "Yes, you can make the green salad, please. I might even let you bake the brownies too if you would not mind doing that for me."

Pasty says, "Of course, I will gladly help."

It was not long before Pauline and Pamela came home from work. They also went upstairs to their bedrooms and changed their clothes. They both put on shorts and a tank top. Once they were done, they headed downstairs so that they could set the dinner table, so they would be able to eat once the dinner was cooked. Peggy was already boiling the potatoes, and she was also frying chicken. Peggy was also waiting for her yeast rolls to finish rising so that she would be able to place them in the oven and bake. Peggy was very happy being in the kitchen cooking a nice meal for her family. Pamela walked into the kitchen and took everything she needs out of the cabinets to set the dining room table for dinner. Once Pamela was all done with that, Pamela noticed that Carl Manning and Jack Marble were talking together in the sunroom. Pamela walked into the living room where Pauline was at, and Pamela told Pauline: Look, our men are in the sunroom together and are talking to each other.

Pauline says: Yes, isn't that sweet, our guys building a good bond with each other.

Soon, dinner was done, and Pasty and Peggy told everyone to please come to the table and enjoy the family meal. Everyone came to the table.

Paul says, "We should say grace."

Peggy smiled and said, "Everyone join hands."

The whole family was standing around the table, and they all joined hands, bowed, and prayed. Once they were done with grace, everyone sat down, and they started their meal. Peggy started the conversation off the girls and talked about work, and the guys were trying to talk about having a surprise party for their girls. They guys came to an agreement on when and where this party should take place. The Williams sisters did not hear what Paul, Mike, Jack Marble, and Carl Manning were talking about. The sisters were so involved with their conversation they totally had no idea that their guys were planning a party.

Once everyone was done eating, they slowly one by one made it to the living room, except for Pauline and Pamela. Pauline and

Pamela cleaned up the kitchen and dining room. Pasty and Mike decided they wanted to spend some alone time together. They both got up from their seat and walked out of the living room, and they headed upstairs to their bedroom, so they could be able to talk directly with each other without other people hearing the conversation. Soon after Pasty and Mike talked about a few things, they decided to go back downstairs and join the rest of the gang. Just as Mike started into the living room, he saw Paul. Mike asks, "Paul, can I talk to you alone, please?"

Paul answers, "Why, yes, you sure can talk to me." Paul stood up and walked where Mike was. He says, "Lead the way."

They started walking toward the back door of the manor, and they walked outside together.

Mike says, I have a big surprise for Pasty on our wedding day right after the ceremony."

Paul says, "Pasty does not know anything about this big surprise that you have planned?"

Mike says, "No, she does not. I want to buy the house next door to the manor. It is for sale. I want us to have our own home. We would be right next door to each other. It should not enter fear with their magical powers at all. What do you think, Paul?"

Paul says, "I personally think it is a good idea, and I am sure that Pasty would enjoy having her own home. Pasty wants to have a family."

Mike says, "Would you go with me tomorrow after work to the real-estate office before five?"

Paul says, "I would be happy to. I can get off from work about three. If you can get off by four, we could meet there."

They both agreed, and they both walked back into the manor. They went back into the living room where everyone was. After they all watched the movie on the television, they all decided they were ready for bed.

Pasty and Mike walked upstairs and went into their bedroom. They set their alarms, so they would be able to get up and get ready for work the next day. Pasty had already picked out her outfit she was going to wear for work tomorrow. She had everything that she would need when she wakes up in the morning so that she could get ready for work. Mike would already be at work. It was not long before Peggy and Paul went upstairs to go to bed. Peggy had her alarm set for seven in the morning, so she would be able to do everything she needed for her family in the morning. Paul walked back downstairs to make sure everything was locked up. Paul went in each room of the manor while he was downstairs, making sure the house was completely safe for his family to lie down and rest. Pauline and Carl Manning went to Pauline's bedroom, and they too set their alarms, so they would be able to get up for work tomorrow. Pamela and Jack Marble went to bed also. Once Paul was completely done downstairs, he proceeded to the attic to check things out there. He wanted to make sure that the book of shadows was safe and protected, so, he set up the alarm with the crystals to protect the book of shadows. As soon as Paul was done with that, he shut the door to the attic and went to his bedroom. He crawled in bed with his wife and found his comfort spot, and off to sweet dreams for him. Now everyone was in bed and fast asleep. They were all having pleasant dreams.

Now the spirit that has been after Peggy for some time was on the prowl in the manor. She wanted to figure out just how to make Peggy go with her when out of nowhere, George Mathis appeared, grabbed the spirit around the neck, and proceeded to apply pressure around it. She could feel the might in his hands and his mind. The spirit did not want to deal with George. She told him that if he wants to hurt the Williams sisters, she would not step in his way.

The spirit told George just as he let go of her and the spirit was ready to vanish you will not succeed in this venture. I will not help you, but I will not stand in your way. The spirit said: You will fail.

The spirit disappeared after saying that to Cole. George was furious with the spirit. He vowed to make the spirit disappear forever.

George was so mad he picked up a crystal vase that was on the dining room table and threw it across the room as he vanished. The noise woke everyone in the manor. Pasty, Mike, Paul, Peggy, Pauline, Carl Manning, Pamela, and Jack Marble all jumped straight up in the air, and they all said at the exact time: Oh my god! What on earth was that?

Everyone jump up out of bed and ran downstairs, and as they came in to the dining room, that is when they saw the crystal vase shattered on the floor. Paul, Mike, Carl Manning, and Jack Marble started looking around the manor to make sure everything else was all right. Pasty went and got the broom and dust pan. Pauline brought the garbage can from the kitchen so that they could put the shattered glass in the trash can. Pamela brought the vacuum cleaner out, and once all the glass was picked up and swept, that is when Pamela ran the vacuum cleaner.

Once the guys knew that the manor was locked up and safe, everyone went back to bed for three more hours before they would have to start getting up for work. Except for Mike and Jack Marble, they had one hour left of sleep before they would have to get up and leave for work.

Peggy woke up just as her alarm went off. She turned her alarm off and quietly got out of bed and walked straight in to their bathroom. Since there was a night light, she shut the bathroom door, turned on the shower light, and took her shower. She was trying her best to be as quiet as possible. Peggy finished getting ready for her day and walked out of the bathroom, turning out the lights before she opens the door. She then walked out of the bedroom and pulled the door shut. Peggy then headed to the kitchen to start coffee and setting out the cereal bowls for breakfast.

Soon, all the Williams sisters were downstairs and, in the kitchen, eating breakfast and drinking their coffee. It was not long before Paul and Carl Manning came downstairs and walked straight to the kitchen, so they would be able to spend a little time with Peggy and Pauline. Pasty, Peggy, Pauline, and Pamela were ready to leave for work. As all the Williams sisters finished their breakfast and they took their dirty dishes to the sink, Peggy and Pauline kissed their men. The other sisters walked to the front door and waited for Peggy and Pauline. Once every one of the sisters walked to the front door, Pasty opened it, and they all walked out to their cars, so they would be able to go to work. Pasty, Peggy, Pauline, and Pamela opened their car doors, got into their cars, put their seatbelts on, and cranked their cars to leave for work. Paul finished his breakfast and went ahead and cleaned up the kitchen. Paul also made sure that the country style ribs was thawing out for dinner. Paul was going to cook ribs on the grill for dinner tonight. Once Paul was all done downstairs, he orbed off to magic school.

Now while everyone was at work and not at the manor, it was a perfect time for George to go to the Williams manor. George was putting the final touches on his plan to kidnap Peggy. George took lots of pictures of the manor. Each room was captured on film so that George would be able to fix the fake Williams manor, and Peggy would not be too suspicious and figure out that she had been kidnapped. George already had the other realm ready, and he was ready to magically create the false Williams manor. George vanished into thin air and went to the other realm and created the fake Williams manor. He could make the fake Williams manor with everything up to the last detail, which was finally in place. Now all George would have to do is wait for the perfect time to kidnap Holly. Now George knew that there was going to be a wedding for Pasty and Mike, and with all the guest who will come to the wedding by the time everything is done pertaining to the wedding and the ceremony when everything was done the Williams family will all be dead dog tired. He decided that on the wedding night, while everyone was sleeping, that would be the perfect time to kidnap Peggy. The Williams family would wake up and wonder where Peggy is. Cole's plan left no room for error. In other words, Cole's plan had to be perfect.

Now everyone had been at work all day, and it was getting close to time for the Williams sisters and their spouse along with their boyfriends. Paul was done for the day, and he orbed home to check and make sure everything was all right. The spirit, however, was up in the attic and unaware that Paul was on his way back to the manor. Paul arrived at the manor. He landed in the kitchen was where he wanted to end up because he wanted a good glass of iced tea.

Paul decided he would check the attic to see if everything was all right. Just about the time Paul was ready to orb to the attic, the spirit was caught in the trap. The alarms went off, and Paul orbed to the attic to find the spirit caught in his trap. Paul started questioning her, and she told Paul just before he let her loose, she would have Peggy with her. The spirit told Paul: There is absolutely nothing you can do about it either.

Paul says: If you think for one moment that the Williams sisters are going to let you take their sister, you better have another thought coming. The Williams sisters will never let you have Peggy. Apparently, you do not know the powers the Williams sisters have. The Williams sisters are good witches, and they will never turn evil. The bond that these sisters have is totally unbelievable. Their bond is strictly love for good never hate for evil. Evil will never reign here in the Williams manor nor will evil destroy what is good in these sisters' lives.

Peggy and Pasty came home from work. They both went upstairs to change into some more relaxing clothes. As soon as Peggy was done changing her clothes, she walked out of her room. Pasty was in the bathroom when suddenly Paul, Peggy, and Pasty heard this gosh-awful scream, and it sounded like it came from the attic. All three of them jumped, and Pasty pulled her shorts up and ran out of the bathroom of her room and saw Peggy running up to the attic. Pasty was right behind her. Paul orbed up to the attic. When Paul arrived, Peggy and Pasty was standing in the doorway of the attic. They all looked inside the attic door, and to their amazement, there was a spirit caught in the trap protecting the book of shadows from being stolen. The spirit that was caught was the one who wanted to have Peggy all to herself. Peggy says: Why are you in my attic near my book of shadows in my trap.

The spirit says: I am here to warn you. Evil is after you. You are in danger. Pure evil is after you, Peggy. You are in very bad danger. Don't forget I warned you. With that, the spirit was out of the trap, and she vanished in to thin air.

Pasty, Peggy, and Paul looked at each other with such a puzzled face, and then they had to explain to Pauline what had happened. Pauline was so shocked it scared her because she took the threat seriously. Pauline says: Peggy, the spirit threatens you, and you aren't worried.

Peggy says: Don't be silly. I am horrified over the thought of this.

Pasty says: Me too. Who does that spirit think she is that she can threaten my sister and get away with it?

Peggy says: I don't like any of this at all. I am scared to death now. I don't feel very safe at all.

Paul says: Don't you worry. I will keep you safe. I won't let anything happen to you.

Chapter 11

Wedding Bells Are Coming Real Soon

It is a beautiful Friday night. All the Williams sisters are home, and Paul, Mike, Carl Manning, and Jack Marble are all sitting in the living room watching television. They are watching a movie that Mike and Pasty rented. Paul had turned out the lights in the manor except for a lamp that was on in the living room. Pasty, Peggy, Pauline, Pamela, Paul, Mike, Carl Manning, and Jack Marble were not aware that the front door of the manor had been opened by George Mathis, who was invisible. He was on his way to the attic to make sure he had all the details of the attic completed and right. George needed to make sure he did not miss any details about what was in the attic. Suddenly, out of nowhere, there was a sound as if doors were being slammed throughout the manor. When the first door slammed, Pasty jumped up and said: What on earth is that?

Peggy says: It sounds like a door being slammed upstairs.

Paul says: Come on, Pamela, let's orb up to the attic and see what the heck is going on. Pamela stood up and orbed to the attic along with Paul. Mike, Jack Marble, and Carl Manning started getting up and walking around the manor on the first floor to check if they could see who it was. Pauline walked up the stairs along with Pasty and Peggy to see if they could find out what was going on. Just as Pauline walked into her bedroom and she walked over to the ole says: I want you to be my queen of darkness.

Pauline says: You are pipe dreaming. This will never happen. Cole, you will can never ever hurt me in our home.

George says: How do you know that I will hurt you?

Pauline says: Don't you worry about it, George. Just know that you will never have the chance to ever hurt me.

The moment Pauline got those words out of her mouth, George disappeared in front of Pauline's eyes. Then she stood up and walked to the bedroom door and saw Pasty standing in her doorway. Pauline said very loudly to Pasty: George Mathis, the district attorney, was just here in my room.

Pasty walked over to Pauline and said: What did he want?

Pauline says: That George Mathis has threatened to do something if I don't marry him.

Pasty says: So, what did you tell him?

Pauline says: I told him he will never have the chance to ever hurt me.

Pasty says: Paul, we all need to orb outside to check and make sure the manor is not being taken apart.

Paul says: Everyone joins hands.

They all joined hands, and Paul orbed them outside. Pasty and Mike walked out back to check the backyard and the back of the manor. Paul and Peggy walked around to the right side of the manor to check it out. Pauline and Carl Manning went to the left side of the manor. Pamela and Jack Marble went to the front of the manor. It seems that the top of the attic was open. Pasty, Mike, Peggy, Paul, Pamela, and Jack Marble walked to front of the manor, and they all saw that the top of the attic was missing. As soon as they all saw the attic was open, they all said: What on earth is going on?

The moment they all got those words out of their mouths, the attic reappeared while this was going on Pasty, Mike, Peggy, Paul, Pauline, Carl Manning, Pamela and Jack Marble were standing there with their mouths hanging open in shock. After they all closed their mouths, Pasty says, "What just happened? Would someone please tell me what just happened."

Peggy says, "Yeah. Exactly what just happened, and why did this happen?

Out of nowhere, George appeared and said, "This is fair warning to all who live in the Williams manor. None of you can stop me from making Pauline my queen of darkness."

Pauline says, "You are very wrong, George. I will never be your queen of darkness or evil."

George was so mad he made the front and back door of the manor explode.

Paul could heal the back door, and Pasty, Mike, Paul, Peggy, Pauline, Carl Manning, Pamela, and Jack Marble all walked back into the manor. Just as they walked into the manor, they heard a very loud noise coming from the attic. Paul orbed up to the attic, and he saw that the roof had reappeared. He walked out of the attic and went downstairs where all the gang was standing. Paul says: The attic roof is back where it is supposed to be.

It was late, and everyone was exhausted, so they all went upstairs excepted for Paul. He walked into the living room, turned off the television, and made sure the doors in the house was locked up.

He then checked on all the windows to make sure they were all closed and locked. Once Paul was done, he decided it was bedtime for him. He walked to his room, got his jammies bottoms on, and crawled into bed and went to sleep.

The dawn was finally breaking, and soon, Peggy would be getting up to start her beautiful weekend. There were lots of things to be done today. Paul and Mike had a lot of things to do today. This was the last weekend before Pasty and Mike would be getting married. This was a joyous occasion not just for Pasty and Mike but for the Williams family as well. This marriage was to unite to soulmates who belong together.

Peggy's alarm went off, and she got up from her bed and walked into the bathroom to take a shower so that she would be ready for her day. Once Peggy was dressed, she walked quietly out of the bathroom, turning out the light before she opened the bathroom door so that it would not wake up Paul as she was leaving the bedroom. Peggy walked downstairs and started heading toward the kitchen when she heard Pasty's voice say: Peggy, wait for me.

Peggy turned around, and she spotted Pasty. They both smiled big at each other. Peggy stopped in her tracks so that Pasty could catch up to her. Pasty and Peggy proceeded to the kitchen. Once they were in the kitchen, Peggy walked over to the coffee pot and pushed the button to start the coffee, and then she walked over to the cabinet that has the coffee cups in it. Peggy proceeded to take out eight coffee cups so that the whole family would be able to enjoy some coffee. She took out all eight bowls so that the family would be able to have cereal for breakfast. Pasty placed all eight bowls on the kitchen counter along with all three boxes of cereal out for the family. Once Pasty was done doing that, she took out eight spoons for the family to eat their cereal. It was not long before everyone was up, and they all had their breakfast and coffee. While they were eating, they had conversations about what their plans were for the day. Pasty and Peggy will be going to the florist to make sure everything was confirmed with the arrangements of the flowers for the wedding of the century. Pauline and Pamela's job were to make sure that the white wicker archway for the bride and groom. Paul and Mike had some business to take care of pertaining to the house that Mike will be purchasing for Pasty and himself to live in after they were married. Carl Manning and Jack Marble were going to clean up the yard and make sure the flower beds did not have any weeds in them. They all finished their breakfast, and everyone was ready to take their day on. They all went on their way to accomplish everything that they needed to get done today. Everyone went on their merry way taking care of all the things that was needed to make sure everything would be ready by next weekend for Pasty and Mike's wedding.

Pasty was so excited about Mike and her making plans for their future. While everyone was not at the manor, George appeared, and he went into Peggy's room and took some of her clothes along with her perfume. Once George had taken everything that he needed to, Peggy would not be able to figure out that she had been kidnapped from the manor. Once George had duplicated everything that was in the real Williams manor, and he was satisfied with everything now, all he needed to do was to wait for the right time to kidnap Peggy.

Soon as every one of the Williams sisters was home and Paul, Mike, Carl Manning, and Jack Marble returned to the manor, Peggy went upstairs to change into some shorts and a T-shirt. Pasty and Mike walked outside with Paul to help him get the grill started so they could all have a cookout for dinner. Peggy had already taken out the steaks to thaw while they were all taking care of the plans for Pasty and Mike's wedding. Pauline went into the kitchen and started cutting up potatoes and boiling eggs along with cutting up celery, onions, pickles, and red bell pepper for her potato salad. Peggy came down stairs walked into the kitchen to get her a glass of fresh tea to drink as she started opening of the two cans of baked beans to go with their dinner. Pasty walked into the kitchen and walked over to the cabinet to get out the plates and the glasses for dinner. She also took out the silverware so that Pamela would be able to set the table. Paul and Mike started cooking the steaks on the grill. Everything was running very smoothly. The Williams sisters got everything ready for dinner. While Pasty, Peggy, Pauline, and Pamela were in the kitchen, Pasty says: You realize we have not had to fight any demons lately?

Peggy says: Every time one of us says that, we end up with a bunch of evil demons wanting to kill us.

Pasty says: You are right sister.

Pauline says: I am grateful for the break from the demons. You would think that the demons would realize they just don't have what it takes to end the Williams sisters.

Pamela says: Personally, I am very glad to have a break from all the evil demons. I love being a witch, but we need a break.

Pasty says: I believe we all love being good witches, and yes, we need a break.

Pamela says: Yes, it makes it hard to have a love life when we are always fighting demons.

Pamela went ahead and set the table, so when dinner was done, they would be able to eat and enjoy their meal. As soon as dinner was over, Pamela and Pauline started cleaning up the kitchen and dining room. Paul and Mike walked outside the backyard where the grill was, so they could clean up all their stuff and bring it in the manor. Once Mike and Paul were all done cleaning up, Paul went into the manor and gathered up all the garbage. He walked it out to the garbage can in the backyard.

Once Paul and Mike were done with the garbage, everyone turned out the lights and shut off the television. They all walked upstairs to them bedrooms and went to bed. Everyone made sure they all had their alarms set so they would be able to get up in the morning and go to work.

Peggy's alarm goes off, and she gets up and walks into the bathroom so that she can get ready for work. Paul was still sleeping, so Peggy always tried her best to be as quiet as possible so that she did not wake up Paul. Pasty was up along with Pauline and Rose. As Peggy finished getting dressed, and she was completely ready for work. She quietly walked out of the bedroom and headed downstairs to the kitchen. Peggy made the coffee. That is when Pauline, Pamela, and Pasty came walking downstairs to go to the kitchen for breakfast and coffee. As soon as everyone was done with their breakfast and coffee, they put their dishes in the sink. As they were walking out the door, they noticed their cars was not in the driveway. Pasty, Peggy, Pauline, and Rose walked back into the manor just as Peggy started to run upstairs to get Paul. Paul came walking into the dining room and ran right into Peggy.

Paul says: Excuse me, I did not see you standing there.

Peggy says: You are not going to believe this, but our cars are gone. They are not in the driveway.

While Pasty, Peggy, Pauline, and Pamela had walked back into the manor, their cars reappeared in the driveway. Paul walked out the front door along with the rest of the Williams sisters. Paul says: I thought you said that your cars were not in the driveway?

Pasty says: Peggy did tell you that because all our cars were gone.

Paul says: Well, apparently, they are not gone because I can see them right in the driveway.

Pasty scratches her head and says: What on earth is going on.

Peggy says: I guess someone is having fun of us.

Peggy gave Paul a kiss, and they all walked over to their cars, got in them, and left for work. Paul was shaking his head. He was very confused. Paul decided since he had to go to magic school, he would have a talk with the elders about who is taking the Williams sisters cars. Once Paul told the elders what was going on, the elders told Paul that all they knew now that evil was lurking around and trying g to figure out a way to hurt the Williams sisters. Paul says: What can we do to stop this evil?

The elders say: Right now, you need to let the Williams sisters know that evil is determined to hurt them. Evil wants to cause the Williams sisters the worst pain ever. Evil insists on trying their best to destroy the Williams sisters.

Paul says: I will not allow evil to win. I will inform the sisters, so they can be on their guard against the evil that is trying to destroy them.

It was not long before Paul left the elders and orbed back to the manor. Paul was very concerned over all the strange things that was happening at the manor. Paul loved each one of the sisters, and he never wanted them to be in harm's way. Paul new that the sisters would need his help in stopping whatever evil was trying to hurt them. Paul went into the kitchen, and he cut up the chicken that Peggy had taken out of the freezer, so he could get it ready for the chicken and rice. It was not long before Pasty and Peggy arrived at the manor. Paul already had poured both Pasty and Peggy a fresh glass of tea with lemon for them to have once they arrive home. As soon as Pasty and Peggy walked in the door and into the kitchen, Paul says: I have poured Pasty and my beautiful wife a good glass of tea.

Pasty and Peggy both looked at Paul and said: Thank you, kind sir.

Paul smiled and said: You two are so sweet. By the way, I cut up the chicken for you, Peggy.

Peggy says: Aww, you are such a good man. Thank you, my sweet, adorable husband.

Peggy washed the chicken and proceeded to make her dinner for her family. As Peggy was in the kitchen cooking, George popped in the manor and grabbed Paul. The next thing Paul knew, he was underground where evil was lurking all around. George says: You can count on me destroy win in the ending your family. I will take glorious pleasure in hurting each one of you.

Paul says: You will never destroy my happy family. George, you will lose. My family has four good witches that fight evil every day, and they always win.

George says: I may die trying to kill each one of you, but my simple pleasure will be watching all of you beg for your lives as I destroy each one of you.

The next thing Paul was back in the manor, and he ran into the kitchen where Peggy was cooking. Paul says: You are not going to believe what just happen.

Peggy says: What happened?

Paul says: That George just took me to where evil reigns, and he has vowed to destroy each one of us. He said that he is going to destroy each one of us and that it would bring him great pleasure to watch us die. I told George that my family has four good witches who fight evil every day, and in the end, they always win.

www.ingramcontent.com/pod-product-compliance
Lightning Source LLC
LaVergne TN
LVHW040153080526
838202LV00042B/3142